A CHANGE OF FORM

Terrence Hammond was born the youngest of six children in Coventry before the war, and now lives in Peterborough.

He left school at fourteen years of age and did a variety of jobs, including seven years in the Army. Eventually he joined the Post Office and was a Postman for twenty two years. From an early age he was an avid reader and lover of History and has traced his ancestry back several centuries.

In the 1960s he won a mature scholarship to Ruskin College, Oxford for two years to study History, Politics and Economics. In the 1980s he was awarded a Degree with Honours by the Open University.

His hobbies are reading, chess, Scrabble, water painting, and ink drawing.

Widowed after forty-five years, he now lives alone but not lonely.

A CHANGE OF FORM

Terrence Hammond

A CHANGE OF FORM

Olympia Publishers
London

www.olympiapublishers.com
OLYMPIA PAPERBACK EDITION

A CIP catalogue record for this title is
available from the British Library

ISBN: 978-1-905513-19-2

This is a work of fiction.
Names, characters, places and incidents originate from the
writers imagination. Any resemblance to actual persons, living or
dead, is purely coincidental.

First Published in 2007

**Olympia Publishers
78 Cannon Street
London
EC4N 6NQ**

Printed in Great Britain

Dedication

I wish to dedicate this book
to the memory of
Kathleen.

If you were to destroy in mankind the belief in immortality, not only love but every living force maintaining the life of the world would at once be dried up.

DOSTOEVSKI

PART 1

Chapter One

I was born in the midwinter of 1324 at a place called Papworth Everard in the County of Huntingdonshire, as Thomas Simon. It was a bitterly cold day and there was thick snow on the ground.

I know because I was there on that day, 4th January, nearly seven hundred years ago. My father, Joseph, was the village blacksmith and he already had a daughter, Kathleen. My mother died two years later producing my other sister Molly.

Left with three small children, my father was obliged to seek help from his extended family: some thirty per cent of the village were related to him in some way. So we all went to live with his married sister in the village.

Some two years later my father remarried. My new mother was a spinster in her early twenties from the Plum family by the name of Judith. Father by now was in his late twenties. I remember quite well all those years ago going to the Church of Saint James. I was far cleaner and smarter than normal and my aunt was nagging me to behave and be quiet. I was feeling happy for the couple and myself. We would be going into our little house that was built by the smithy and would be a happy family in less crowded conditions. From here on things were going to be different with no aunt to nag me all the time.

Over the next few years things did turn out differently. Judith gave birth to three daughters in three years. Mary in 1329, Judith in 1330, and Hellen in 1331. Judith now thought she had the right to nag and discipline me. Molly thought it might help to ingratiate herself with our stepmother if she told tales about me, true or false. Kathleen on the other hand was usually on my side.

Such was the clutter and crowding in our house that one day when agitation seemed to be building up with the adults, I was able to conceal myself in a corner and from my hiding place to observe the birth of my half-sister, Hellen. I was at first frightened then fascinated. Living in a village full of animals I had seen animals give birth but thought humans were different. How on earth did females get babies in their stomachs anyway and if it was so painful why did they do it repeatedly? The problem was to worry me for the next seven years.

Our house only had two rooms, one for us six children. With all that chatter and noise from five girls, I volunteered to sleep in the smithy with the horse. It was warmer and quieter. Father agreed and I made a bed of sorts under a bench in the corner and imagined I would be free from marauding rats, chickens, cockroaches and evil imps.

Another advantage was that I could urinate in the horse stall away from inquisitive girls, for I was a modest boy. There was yet another advantage as I grew older: I could go out into the night without being noticed.

My father naturally wanted me to follow in his footsteps, for there was a steady living to be made by a blacksmith on the main road to Huntingdon some seven miles away in addition to the normal trade in the village. So from an early age I was expected to help out in the smithy learning the trade and earning my keep.

Judith was a bit on the religious side and insisted we all go to church on a Sunday. She also thought that as the only boy I should be taught to read, if not write. My father supported her and said he could read and write and it was an advantage. I had not however seen any parchments or books around the house. In fact, I had never seen a book though I was told the priest had one. I also thought that in any case it had not done him much good because he still had to work in that hot smithy six days a week. At times he seemed to work harder than the ignorant labourers in the fields.

Anyway, twice a week I was sent with three or four other boys to a little old lady who taught very little because she didn't know much herself and she could not keep us in order. At that time I was not interested in learning my letters as it seemed that it would be of no use to me in the future.

Some nights in the good weather I would sneak out and join my friend John Ingram who was the youngest son of the carpenter and slept in his father's woodshed. Sometimes the pair of us would go down to the spinney and catch a rabbit. We left the carcass on the doorstep so that our parents wouldn't know we had been out. They apparently thought some well-wisher had left them and us boys got rabbit for dinner.

18

John complained that he always got the smallest portion. Sometimes the fox got to the doorstep first and we got nothing for out troubles.

While quite young all us boys were introduced to archery. The squire and the church warden were both self-proclaimed experts, and we were put under the tutelage of Ian Moore, an ex-soldier. We were divided up into groups by age and were given much advice and encouragement on the butts behind the church. I found this good sport and never missed a training session or competition. I certainly liked it better than learning my letters. Another of my favourite pastimes was playing football. My father objected whenever he found out and claimed some recent King had forbidden it because it interfered with archery practice. Actually father objected to it because I played with labourers' sons and might be getting wrong ideas and wasting time that could be spent in his smithy. When I turned up muddy and worn I merited a clip round the ear and a telling off for the rest of the day. For some reason he did not object if he thought I had been fighting with other boys, which was not often.

While I was quite young my father let me ride his horse, which was fun. When he thought I was proficient enough he would send me on errands to his customers, which brought me into contact with a wide range of people.

Being an only son with my own sleeping place in our abode, the only village boy that could ride a horse with skill and confidence, plus the fact that I could write my own name gave me a certain confidence and arrogance with other boys. I was also an attraction to girls as I grew older but knew not how to deal with them.

I was not generally involved or interested in my string of sisters and kept away from them as much as possible. Molly was always trying to cause trouble with me but Judith now listened less and less. My elder sister always stuck up for me, she thought that as an only boy I was something special. I spent more time in the smithy with father than with the rest of the family put together.

My first serious encounter with the female sex was when I was seventeen. I was riding out of St Ives, having been there on my father's business, when I came across Joan Earnshaw from our village also heading for home; she was on foot. By now I knew more about females from talk with other boys and was hoping soon to put into practice the things I had heard about for it had fired my imagination. As I came closer I hailed her.

"Hullo Joan! Are you going home?" What a silly question but I had to say something.

"Hullo Tom! Yes I'm on my way to Papworth."

She was carrying a wicker basket with things in it. She looked a bit worn and footsore but she was at sixteen years of age quite buxom.

"Would you like a lift on my horse?"

I had drawn up alongside and had a good view of just how buxom she was.

"Oh No! But thank you for the offer."

"Why not? You are already worn out and there is still five miles to go."

"My father would kill me if he found me riding horseback with a young man. It is not a thing a girl can do without people talking."

I laughed, "I am not some stranger just passing through or a squire's son. I am a neighbour you have known since childhood."

We both stopped and smiled at each other.

"Anyway I could not climb up on that great thing."

A thrill ran through me. The *no* was gone, it was *how*.

"Get yourself up on that fence and it will be easy."

We moved over to the fence and I dismounted to hold the horse while she got astride him. Watching her swing a leg over and fiddling with her cumbersome skirt set my pulse racing faster. I climbed up behind her and with one hand supporting her and the other guiding the horse we set off. I could feel straight away why her father had been concerned.

She was overwhelming: her young lithe body bouncing up and down against me. It was not very long before my hand was on her breast. The wicker basket kept getting in the way, but where there is a will there is a way.

Two miles down the road I stopped before I did myself a mischief. I dismounted and lifted her down on the excuse that the horse needed a rest. Standing up close to her as she dismounted was even more overwhelming. I wrapped her in my arms and kissed her on the lips as best I knew how. This was different to anything I had known before and I needed both hands – the horse could look after itself for once.

But I was not going to get far with this new kind of fun. Soon there were loud cries and curses from a passer-by as my horse ambled across the narrow road. Though I was much afraid that Joan might change her mind if I let her go, I was compelled to collect my horse. I tied the horse to a tree and intended to get off the road out of sight with Joan; she seemed willing enough.

But it was not to be. A voice hailed Joan. A neighbour and his wife rattled up the in the squire's horse and cart.

"Come along Joan, jump up here. You must be worn out with all that walking. Your father will wonder where you have got to."

Joan could hardly refuse. In a minute she was gone leaving me to calm down and mount up alone. I wished the neighbour and his wife to hell. But a fire had been lit.

I had time to see Joan several times after that and we sometimes managed a kiss or a bit more. But I was worried about being seen in close contact with a girl and she was worried about other things. What with archery practice, riding errands for father and long hours at the smithy I didn't get much time to pursue Joan. As time went on, other girls caught my eye. One of these that later stood out was Isobel Plum; she was a good-looking daughter of an Ostler and was more available because she was a relative via my stepmother. I did not have much success with her at first and she was not too keen. Things got better over time; people noticed and seemed to approve.

In the year 1344 when I was twenty years old and growing increasingly frustrated with females and the smithy, the Squire died and the young Harold Hodge, only a year older than I, succeeded to his father's lands, properties and his knighthood. We had often spoken in a friendly manner when we met.

One day as I rode along the road we met. I stopped to let him pass at a narrow spot and doffed my hat, for he was master now of all this neighbourhood. I offered him my condolences after we had acknowledged each other although we had all been obliged to attend his father's funeral service and commiserate with him at the time it did no harm to do it again alone, for one had to keep well in with the top dog. Now, however, I got presumptuous.

"How are you coping with running the manor, sir?"

"That is no problem. I have a bailiff to cope with most of it and a farm manager. Mother looks after the domestic side so all told I have a lot of spare time. I might be the Squire and a knight to boot but it is all show. I want to do something useful in the county."

I was much surprised that he had confided so much in me, he must be a lonely man.

"What have you in mind?" I asked. Who was I to question my social superior, but there, it was out. After all we had known each other since childhood and I had often been to the manor house on my father's business.

"Well," he said as the horses became restless, "I have been asked to organise an archery competition at the Great Annual Fair in Huntingdon which will be followed by some jousting. It could bring me to the notice of some important people. I need to take up the military side of knighthood if I can find a suitable instructor. Father was never into that and preferred to pay the scutage."

I assured him all would be well and sorted out to his satisfaction given a little time. Then he came out with a surprise question.

"I say Tom, I hear you are very good at archery. Why don't you come along and compete in the competition at Huntingdon?"

I was struck with apprehension at having to compete at such a level – how would I fare against the experts – but I was also delighted to be asked. I mumbled something but he pressed the point so I tentatively agreed. After all it was a long time off and he was the Squire.

On my return to Papworth I sought out Ian Moore and told what the Squire said. He was of the opinion that I should go.

"You and John Ingram are the best archers in the village. You should both try your hand at county level; I'll help as much as I can."

John was much surprised when he was informed that we were going to compete at county level.

The females in the family were proud that I had been selected though Molly could not resist the odd sarcastic remark. Father was not happy, there was work to be done in the smithy and he was not getting any younger. The one person who was really pleased was Isobel. We now became much closer friends.

In the autumn my sister Kathleen married John Hollow and went off across the village to her new home.

As the year wore on Isobel and I became much taken up with each other and in January I proposed to her in front of St James

Church. She said 'yes' with a big smile. But of course we had to have the approval of her parents, which they gladly gave.

Isobel was a year younger than I. Once both families were in favour the date was set, 20th March 1345. The main task before the wedding was to build a house for ourselves on my father's land next to the smithy. All sorts of people came along to help us, not just relatives. Isobel's main problem as the day approached was to keep my hands off her for she had become very tempting.

Once the day arrived we were as happy as could be.

Father was a bit disgruntled in the aftermath. I preferred to be with my new wife or honing my skill at archery than being in his smithy, but one has to earn a living.

As time went on more and more was required of me in the smithy, sometimes I was even left in charge. I learnt to live with my wife as well as horse riding and archery and to hate the smithy.

Then came the time for the archery contest at the Great Annual Fair. I rode to Huntingdon in the company of Sir Harold and Ian, while John trotted behind.

The competition was to be held in a field behind the castle on the opposite side of the river.

We would be there in tents for approximately two days. All sorts of people swarmed out to see us. There were two score or more of us archers. Throughout the morning we gathered, were organised into teams and allocated our tents. We chatted and laughed together unaware of the talent spotters. After a sumptuous dinner the serious business began. We were in teams of six. Our team did very well and ended up in the top two; tomorrow we would find out who was the champion team. After a break for refreshment we then had the individual contests. I ended up in the top four. There was everything to play for tomorrow. I was very pleased with myself and the team. John had been knocked out of the individual finals but he had done well.

That night there was much jollity in our camp and across the main road; over there were girls as well as beer. I stayed in the camp by the fire talking until rather late; I did not drink much for I would need my wits and concentration about me in the morning. With Isobel waiting for me at Papworth I had no need of female company.

Next day our confidence was dented. We were now in a different league, the shooting was of a very high order, there was much cheering and hooting. Most of my family including Isobel were in the audience as well as other people from Papworth.

My team went down. In the individual contests I came third. We had not disgraced ourselves and I was well pleased with the final outcome.

After a few words with Isobel and father they set off home while I went back to the team.

As we were packing up in the early evening to go home Sir Harold called me out for a private chat.

"I have been watching you very closely of late, Tom, and I am very pleased with you."

I was duly flattered and pleased but wondered why he had not called John out as well. He was a tenant of Sir Harold the same as I and had shot well against strong opposition. Then came the reason.

"I am going in Huntingdon Castle for some proper training as a knight. I have also agreed to enlist and be available should, or when, the war with France flares up again."

He paused for effect. So he was planning to go to war and leave the Manor to be run by his bailiff. What did that mean for me? Why should he single me out to tell me his business – he was a knight and I was the son of a blacksmith. He then continued.

"As a knight bachelor I must have a full lance to go on campaign that means one squire, one man at arms and three mounted archers at a minimum." There was another pause as I felt his eye boring into me. "I would like you to enlist with me as one of my archers. What do you think of that? The pay is six pence a day." I was speechless.

"Think it over Tom and let me know in the next few days."

I regained my composure.

"Well Sir Harold, first of all I haven't got a horse; it belongs to my father and is not too fit. Also I could not afford the various items to get started and last but not least I am married." Let him get round that. An outright refusal would not have been in my long term interests, I have never thought of being a soldier.

"Well there is no reason why your wife should not come along. You can both have quarters in Huntingdon for the rest of the year. I can provide you with a horse and any necessities." He paused for a while for he had noticed my reluctance. After the carrot came the stick.

24

"Think of this. If it comes to a major war with France, every able-bodied man between sixteen and sixty years of age will be liable for military service. The days of feudal armies might be over, but the King will want lots of men. As an able-bodied man and a competent archer you will almost certainly be impressed by the Commissioners of Array. You would find yourself a foot soldier at two pence a day. Think of that."

He could see he had left me a little nonplussed. My life up to now had been directed to me being a blacksmith. Archery and riding were pleasant pastimes. Now the Lord of the Manor was talking of something very different.

I rode back to Papworth with Ian. As we clattered across the bridge over the Great Ouse and away from the castle I told him what Sir Harold had said.

"That is as good an offer as you are likely to get. Do you want to be a blacksmith all your life? Do you want to serve with common men at the bottom of the heap marching all over the place?" He had touched a soft spot. "You are a very good archer and you can ride. There is adventure waiting out there for such as you."

"I'll think about it," I said.

"Well don't take too long. Sir Harold is waiting."

The rest of the way home we rode in silence. When I arrived at home Isobel was waiting with some news for me. She was pregnant. That gave me more to think about.

I raised the matter of military service with my father. He was most indignant and upset that I even considered the matter, my place was in the smithy. The thought of sweating and labouring away for thirty years in his hot smithy while the world rolled by had the opposite effect to what he intended. Mother was noncommittal. I went to see my sister Kathleen; she was much in favour. Like Ian she thought it would be ideal for me and it was not for ever. I was too restless to stay in the village; Isobel would go with me anywhere.

I went back to Isobel. I had told her before anyone but it had not sunk in, her mind was much taken up with being pregnant. Now she had had time to think. As we talked in the flickering light of a torch it was like Kathleen had said, she was willing to go anywhere where I wanted. She had noticed how I was getting irritable at father's carping and she used the same words as Ian.

"Do you want to be a blacksmith all your life? You must do what you are best at. You will not be happy tied to an anvil for life." So it was agreed before we snuggled down in the straw together.

Next morning after breakfast, with father grumbling and rather distressed, I walked to the Manor to see Sir Harold. The die was cast.

On the way back I met John and told him my decision.

"I would like a chance like that," he said. "But I cannot ride. I wish you the best of luck Tom." We clasped hands then silently went on our way.

Within a week I had a new high-spirited horse that I found at first rather hard to handle – but I mastered him. He would remain in the Manor but be available to me at any time I chose.

In the trip to Huntingdon the three of us (me, Isobel and the horse) carried all our worldly possessions with ease. The house was locked up and away we went on this new adventure together.

At Huntingdon we lodged with a friendly widow, a Mrs Rodgers. A partition was erected across the single room. In our half was a bed of straw, an overturned box for a table and one stool. There was no sound barrier between us and Mrs Rodgers.

Next day at the castle I was given a steel helmet, a padded jacket with an emblem on it, a new bow with twenty-four arrows and a dagger with a nine-inch blade. My horse was quartered in the castle in a stall better than mine. The other two archers of the lance were Leonard Roper and Peter Turner, both had been in the team with me at Huntingdon. Both were good archers.

Every day we were put to practicing archery, riding and other duties. If the weather was too bad we did close quarter combat in the castle. We grew close together as comrades and as a fighting unit. We were integrated with all the other lances, knights and foot soldiers as a combat-effective team. We met many interesting new friends, went to various tournaments and contests. In short, we thoroughly enjoyed ourselves.

All this time Isobel got bigger.

As the year drew to a close we all thought we were in some sort of golden age. In fact the devil had us in his grip.

With the coming of winter much activity was curtailed. Many men went home to villages and towns a day's ride away. To those of us who stayed our commanders tried to keep us occupied. Not only was there indoor military training, wrestling competitions etc, but some of the commanders such as our Sir Harold thought it would be a good time to improve our writing and reading abilities, in order to understand things better. Some commanders thought this would be dangerous.

In December, nine months after we were married Isobel gave birth to a fine healthy son. Mrs Rodgers and her sister were indispensable at this time. We named him John and he was christened in the castle chapel. Leonard and Peter stood as his Godfathers and Mrs Rodgers as his Godmother.

There was little doubt in our minds that despite all the efforts of the French and the Pope to extend the armistice we were heading for a major war. My comrades and I were pleased at the prospect. As the winter receded and we approached Lady Day, Commissioners of Array were sent out all over the country to impress eligible young men for service in the English army. War it was to be.

In later April 1346 I said goodbye to my wife and baby son. With Sir John Silk as our knight bannerette, some one hundred and fifty of us with many others set off at the King's command to Portsmouth.

The weather was not too good as we rode or marched along muddy roads; the nights were cold as we slept more often in the open. But we were happy as we went on through Luton, Reading and Winchester. We passed around Portsmouth onto Southsea Common where a large tented camp awaited us.

All told there must have been twenty thousand of us gathered on that common. Not all were English; there were a number of Welsh and a smattering of Irish. There were many from nobility there. The King had already informed Parliament that he was going to take his force to Gascony.

If we thought we would go straight on our ships and off to the south of France we were sadly mistaken. We waited week after week for the wind to change. Camping out there on the common looking down on Spithead which was full of ships waiting to transport us it was difficult to fill our time and there was some friction between us.

Locals told us of the insolent French who had come raiding, looting and burning along our shore and of innocent people murdered by these evil men. Vows were made to take vengeance.

Then I met an old friend; we greeted each other like long lost brothers. It was John.

"How on earth did you get here?" I asked him.

"I was impressed," he said cheerfully. "A good archer, fit as a butcher's dog and a youngest son. The Commissioners thought I was a gift."

We embraced each other. John was a foot archer and looked down upon by us mounted regulars. Nevertheless I introduced him to my little circle of friends and we had many happy evenings together.

The embarkation began as the wind changed direction. On 5th July we sailed with much jubilation. But not far. The wind blew up and storms came. We were compelled to anchor to the lee of the Isle of Wight off St Hellen's Point just across the Spithead. There we spent the best part of a week bobbing about in those crowded little ships. Many were seasick and all were sodden and miserable.

At last, on the 11th, we moved off following the King out into the Channel. Once out of sight of land our commanders opened sealed orders and called us together.

"We are not going to Gascony to aid our countrymen! We are going to Normandy just across the Channel. From there we shall march on Paris!"

There was loud cheering. Normandy might be in the north away from sunny Gascony but the lure of Paris and only one night at sea instead of the expected week sent spirits soaring.

Frenchie here we come!

Chapter Two

On the 12th July we landed in Normandy at the port of St Vaast. We could see from the flags and banners where the King was.

"There is something going on over there, let us go and have a look," said Len.

So the three of us moved through the milling soldiers to get a better view of what was going on.

"The King is knighting a lot of people over there; shall we go and join the queue?" I asked. That brought a laugh from those around. Though the scene was quite fascinating we could not stay for long for there was work to do and Sir Harold would be looking for us.

For the next five days we were busy disembarking all our horses, wagons, tents and stores. Until our tent was erected we slept under the stars.

There was no sign of the French army and their fleet kept away from our superior naval force.

Reconnaissance parties were dispatched to frighten the locals and to collect information and supplies.

"Can we go?" we asked Sir Harold as soon as we had our horses. We wanted to be out and about having fun.

"No you will not go, you will stay right here until we get orders!"

So we stayed put feeling boxed up while others rode forth. The camp site was not too healthy and soon began to smell of horse manure and latrines.

On the 18th our whole army was ready to move. The Earl of Warwick and his division was the first to go followed by the King's division and the supply train. Then under the Earl of Northampton we brought up the rear. We were not very happy with that but before we set off Sir John addressed us.

"Don't worry my lads about being in the rear, on the day we meet the French army we shall be upfront like everyone else. In the meantime we can spread out more than Warwick's men and forage further afield. There should be some rich pickings for us." He paused and pulled a parchment out. He cast an eye over us, cleared his throat then began to read to us from the parchment.

"'The King commands that nobody shall set fire to towns, or manors, nor will they rob churches and holy places. Nor will they do harm to civilians, to the aged or the women and children in his realm of France. Anyone who brings to the King such transgressors of his law will receive a reward of fifty shillings.'"

"He's a bit late saying that," said somebody nearby who had already been out foraging.

With further admonishment not to stray away from our comrades and to listen to the commands of our superior officers, we set off behind the rest of the army.

In riding out behind our advancing army but more spread out, there were indeed easy pickings. With the rumours of violence and arson going ahead of us most farmers and peasants, let alone traders, had fled leaving us free to scoop up anything we wanted to carry off or consume. A few farms and villages that had showed resistance or insolence had been ravaged and burnt thus accelerating the exodus of civilians who thought they might be in reach of our foragers. We fed well and filled our sacks with loot. Those of us on horseback were best off, we could range further and carry off more. Yet at no time did I see violence committed against civilians, most had fled or were in hiding.

Then we came to the town of Carentan; large areas of it were on fire with smoke billowing everywhere.

"I thought we were not supposed to do things like that," I said.

"Most murders and arson are done by people from the south coast who have old scores to settle," replied Peter.

"They are not Englishmen doing most of it. There are a lot of wild Welsh and barbarian Irish with us," added Len.

"Well I think their commanders should get a grip of them. Collecting plunder is one thing but arson and murder should be stamped out as the King has ordered," I said rather huffily.

"It has always been thus in war," declared Len.

So we went on down the Cotentin Penisular to the town of St Lo, from there we turned towards Caen, all places we soldiers had never heard of before. As we approached the latter place we closed in to form one long column.

Ten miles from the city we halted, the city and garrison had defied us. The King ordered us to rest and eat while he worked out a plan.

Then Sir John rode up to us.

"Right lads we have got our first fight. We are going to join Warwick's command to assist in the storming of the enemy at St Pierre Bridge. Follow me!"

So we rode in a column past lines of our troops who had just stormed into the old town. To our left was the castle with the French flag flying and their soldiers on the wall watching. They did nothing.

We followed some of Warwick's men through the streets of the old town to the bridge. Along the whole of the west and north side of the town the assault was launched. The enemy held their positions and fought back stoutly.

I had never heard such noise before. The shouting of men, clang of weapons and cries of the horses echoed through the streets. We archers dismounted and looked for places where we could bring our weapons to bear on the enemy. At this point our men were driven back causing much confusion and chaos. The enemy did not follow so we reorganised for another assault. We archers of Sir John's command took station on the flanks of the assault force at the bridge and shot at any of the enemy that showed themselves.

Then we heard a roar of triumph from beyond the wall. Our men had crossed the river and were converging on the bridge.

The French broke and fled out of the town with our knights pursuing them and slaying most of those they caught. At this stage some of our ships came up the Orne from Ouistrehan to the city, destroying enemy ships in the river. Looting in the city now became widespread. I did not miss my share.

"There you are," said Len. "We have had our first fight with the French. Not too bad was it? We are veterans now." We all agreed with him.

When order was restored, worthwhile prisoners and our sick and wounded were put aboard the ships and despatched to England.

We stayed in Caen for five days, sleeping under roofs in soft beds eating captured food. Lovely! Some civilians were rounded up and set to burying the enemy dead of which there were many. Our own dead we dealt with after a short service from the chaplains.

It was nice in Caen. I had never slept in a stone-built house before.

John Ingram was nearby and spent much time with our lance. We decided to teach him to ride so that he could become a mounted archer. He was making good progress when some of his friends turned up and jeered at his efforts. He became rather clumsy and the horse threw him. He lost his confidence and would not go on.

On the 31st July the advance began again. On we went through the brooding countryside. Many were asking "Where is the French army?" The more optimistic asked, "How much further to Paris?"

After seven days of marching we reached the broad waters of the Seine. We evidently planned to cross at Elbeuf but the bridges were down and a large French force scowled at us from across the river. So we moved up river in the direction of Paris while we several times tried to cross the Seine. By now we all knew that Paris was dead ahead, so why did we want to cross the river?

"We could out march the French and be in Paris before they could lock their daughters up," declared Len. "So why are we concerned about crossing over?"

"Our commanders, especially the King, know what they are doing so don't worry. Their daughters are probably as ugly as sin," I told him.

Each time we approached a bridge we found it was down and an ever larger French army on the other side. We in Sir John's command were in action at Meudal when we tried, with the bulk of the army, to force a crossing and were thrown back with loss.

After that Prince Edward was despatched ahead to raid and burn along the southern edge of Paris. This frightened the enemy who marched off quickly to their capital thus leaving an opening for us at Passy. Though the bridge was down only a few Frenchmen guarded it. Strong parties of our men got across and drove the enemy away.

The carpenters and pioneers were then set to work to repair the bridge while many of us worked as labourers to speed things up and get the rest of the army over before the French fell upon us. To our surprise the enemy did nothing.

"I think it is a trap," said Len. "In any case we are going in the wrong direction: both Paris and the French army are over there," he said pointing up the river.

"You are wrong Leonard Roper," declared Sir Harold riding up at that moment. "We have outwitted the French, we have come across the river to join up with the Flemish army which will make us strong enough to fight and beat the French. So stop trying to be a strategist and attend to your own business!"

The rebuke did not stop Len.

"Well where are these Flemish?"

But Sir Harold had already ridden on out of earshot.

Now was began a rapid march to the River Somme. We had a two day march on the enemy but some of our men and horses were beginning to show signs of strain. Len's horses became crippled, two of Sir Harold's were also virtually on their last legs.

"Now what do I do? If I get a lift on somebody else's horse that will soon bring their horse to ruin. I don't favour walking all the way to Picardy to meet the Flemish then all the way to Paris. I wasn't built for walking." Len was getting worried.

"Leave it to us," said Sir Harold. "You keep going with the rest, it'll do you good. Tom and Peter will come with me off the line of march where we should find some horses, I'll see Sir John then we'll be away."

So off we went at right angles to our army. We soon discovered it was a waste of time. The French army had passed by and taken those worth taking. We were compelled to stop and think again.

"If we go a further day's ride out then turn on the same course as the army to Abbeville we should find something," I suggested.

"Yes. I'm afraid we are going to have to cast the net a little wider," he agreed.

So off we went twenty strong. In a couple of hours further riding from our army we came upon what we were looking for: a farmhouse and several huts. Two horses were stood there for the taking, three more were being ridden off by civilians. They stood no chance, Peter and I rode them down. When they protested Peter stabbed and wounded one of them and I shouted and threatened the others. They jumped off and fled.

"Now they know that we are about we shall have to move quickly and in a different direction," declared Sir Harold.

"Look what I have found!" shouted one of our companions. He had two young women who had not run away fast enough. He had one by the arm and the other by the hair of her head. They began screaming.

"Merci! Merci!"

Some of our men began to gloat and let their intentions be known. We had not seen young women for a long time.

"Let those women go!" shouted Sir Harold, spurring his horse towards the trio. Peter and I moved in support.

"We haven't got time for them now. It is horses we want, not French fillies. Release them now!"

The man was struck silent but still agitated, others moved ominously. Sir Harold laid his hand on the hilt of his sword. It was enough. The man released them and stood shamefaced as the two women scuttled away.

"We cannot hang about round here, we must keep moving." Somebody said, "We could have taken the women along with us for later." But Sir Harold never heard him and quickly got us on our way.

We had more success further on then camped for the night in an abandoned farmhouse. The occupants had departed leaving us much food. In the morning we had fresh eggs for breakfast. We moved on just after sunrise. We had more luck in the morning as we turned towards our army. Twice we ran into people driving their horses, cattle and wagons away from our army into our arms. We caused consternation. Men, women and children screamed and ran in all directions. They had heard some fearsome tales about us. We rounded up the horses, looted the wagons and moved on.

By evening we were back in the column again with five good horses and a wagon load of loot just for our lance.

Our army pressed on at a good pace for the best part of a week from the Seine to the Somme intending to cross between Abbeville and Ameins and join the Flemish army, but we were in for a shock. Not only were the bridges down but the main French army with its so-called King was already in Ameins with more French at Abbeville.

"I don't believe it!" declared most of our commanders. "We had a two day start on them, moved with alacrity and they end up in front of us!"

"Well that is what the scouts of the Earl of Warwick tell us. Could they be wrong?" I queried. It was a question many asked. We stopped at a little town of Araines while the King got confirmation and decided what to do next. It was a chance for worn out men and horses to rest. By now some knights were riding old nags and cart horses. My horse was in reasonably good condition, but I had to keep a sharp eye on him as some people were looking his way.

"Where the devil are the Flemish?" was on everyone's lips. Things did not look too good, the French were gathering.

Then off we went again heading west to Oisemont then we formed a single column and turned towards the river downstream from Abbeville. Surely there were no bridges down there?

On the 24th we marched to the river in the early morning and reached its banks near Blanchetaque at daybreak. There we stopped in a long column until mid morning Warwick's men then stepped into the river. There was a ford!

It was not very wide; only a dozen men abreast with archers in the front set off.

Several thousand French could be seen gathering on the far bank one and a half miles away.

"The King must be mad," I heard Sir John say.

We all watched in apprehension as the column snaked out across the river into the jaws of the enemy. Their Genoese archers began firing at the close packed and exposed column. It seemed an age before our men replied. Then all bedlam broke loose as the French knights fell on the head of the column. We could not see clearly what was happening, there was so much splashing about. Then we lost all sight of the struggle as we moved forward down the bank.

"Might as well drown as burn," said Len as we entered the water.

Over we went with all the rest, Northampton's banner leading the way. We were most surprised to see as we approached the opposite bank that our men had thrown the enemy back. Once across we followed our leaders to the right, the enemy here was in full flight to Abbeville being chased by our knights. We followed at a slower pace then gave up and returned to the crossing point.

On the other flank, Warwick's men had gone as far as Crotoy where they burnt French ships before returning.

The last of our wagons was about to cross when the main body of the enemy arrived behind them. Some of our wagons were captured but the enemy did not press the matter: the tide had begun to turn and we were in strength on the north bank. We watched the French turn away to Abbeville.

There was no doubt we had won a spectacular success. We had crossed the Somme on a narrow front under enemy fire then stumbled ashore under attack from the knights and put them all to flight.

We were in high spirits. God was obviously on our side and our King was a master of war. Neither would allow this army to be defeated. If the French wanted a battle now then they could have it.

Moving slowly north on the following day our leaders were looking for a place to stand and fight. There was now no natural barrier between us and the Flemish. But where were they?

"Who cares? We can beat the French on our own," Len had swung from pessimism to optimism as a result of the Somme crossing.

Our leaders next day found the place they were looking for. We all took up positions near the village of Crecy to await the arrival of the French army. Would they accept battle? Throughout the campaign they had been hesitant. We were in no rush, it had been a long trek but now we were ready.

Warwick was on the right, we under Northampton were on the left, the King with the third division was drawn back in the centre as a reserve. The baggage train was behind that. The two forward divisions were covered on their flanks by wedges of archers a little forward of the main line so they could enfilade the advancing enemy. In front of the archers, stakes were hammered into the ground to impede the enemy cavalry. Between the two divisions were lines of Welsh spearmen to cover the steep terrace where no serious attack need be expected. The King himself was in the windmill on the right which gave a perfect view across the valley in front and along the English lines. Extra arrows were now issued from the stocks held in the wagons to supplement the minimum of twenty-four held by each archer. With a bowman launching ten shafts a minute their personal stock would not last long.

When all was in position the King reviewed his army, passing along the ranks on a white palfrey with a short white stick in his hand. Occasionally he halted to give a few words of encouragement.

By midday we were settled down but the French were nowhere in sight. A meal was prepared and the King gave orders for all to relax and eat. Everyone marked his place before going off. Afterwards they stood about talking to comrades.

"Well what do you think of the chances of a major battle today?" I asked.

36

"Pretty slim, the French are not stupid, our position is too strong. Like us they want to fight at an advantage," replied Len.

"Well they will have to do something," declared Peter.

"If they have any sense they will pass across our left to get between us and the Flemish and compel us to attack them," said somebody.

"They don't have to do anything, we will soon run out of supplies cooped up here. When they move they can jump us. I don't suppose they will think of that," was my opinion.

"When the French see us lined up they will be at us like a bull at a red rag. You'll see," said Sir Harold.

"Well they are taking a long time to get here," said Len.

"I'll bet a week's pay they will attack us as soon as they see us," said I. Len accepted the bet and we clasped hands on it. His view was that the French had been over-cautious and would continue to be so. Other bets were made.

At that point a rain squall from out of nowhere came, that sent us archers dashing off to protect out bowstrings. It soon passed over.

When we gathered again Peter was willing to bet there would be no battle today. Sir Harold and I took him on.

It was soon after Vespers in the late afternoon that the French were spotted from the Windmill. Trumpets sounded to be repeated all along the line and we all rushed excitedly to our places. There must have been something like ten thousand fighting men lined up and ready.

For an hour we watched the French emerging before us in great force against our right wing. We were not too worried for we could see they were not very organised, in fact to us they looked more like a noisy mob rather than an affective war machine. Their ranks were hopelessly ragged and out of dressing to do anything militarily effective. The leading force deployed at an angle to approach Warwick's men. We all watched silently as they became more disorganised.

The Genoese archers were up front and now began to ascend the slope on our right shooting off the odd bolt as they came, all fell short. When they were one hundred and fifty paces away sharp words of command rang out among the English and immediately a shower of arrows was released into the air to strike the Genoese with devastating effect. At the same time there was a number of thunder claps and

37

belches of flame. Through the air hurled balls of iron and stone striking down all who got in the way. This was King Edward's secret weapon. The cannon had made its first appearance on an English battlefield and I was there when it happened.

The iron barrels had been boxed up and concealed until required. Not that they did much damage and most people did not notice them in all the noise.

The French knights behind the Genoese pushed to the front and charged towards the English line. Behind them we would see emerging another great column deploying to the right of their comrades and coming towards us.

"I think we have visitors," said Len.

"Then let us give them a warm reception," I replied.

The enemy attack was not co-ordinated. As those attacking Warwick were repulsed the other lot came for us.

"My God," I murmured to myself as the French force, all mounted, all in armour, flags and banners waving, came thundering towards us. We waited in silence until Sir John at a signal from Northampton screamed out in unison with others.

We then shot at the French like we were demented. They swerved away to attack our men at arms leaving us to pour a relentless fire into their exposed flanks. They reeled away leaving men and horses littering the ground in front of us. That was not the end but the beginning.

More French appeared, to launch their attacks on us. Though they faced us all along both wings each group seemed to do their own thing allowing us to concentrate on each group that came forward.

We were using arrows at a tremendous rate and in the pauses some of our men raced forward to retrieve them while their comrades covered them.

The sun was setting behind us and still they came.

"I bet there was never a battle like this before," said Len as the mound of dead and dying men and horses grew before us.

"Well you will have something to tell your grandchildren won't you," I replied.

"None of us will see our grandchildren if we run out of arrows," said Peter.

Night descended and still they came on in the moonlight and we shot them down and retrieved our arrows, often wrenching them from fallen men and horses. At the end of one interval Len nipped back into our ranks and tossed me a small leather bag. I looked inside.

Gold!

"Wherever did you get this?" What a stupid question.

"There is a lot of it out there."

"You were out there to get arrows not gold! Run out of arrows and all the gold in the world will not help you!" shouted Sir Harold.

"Yes I got a load of arrows and I know where the gold is."

"Once we have won this battle you can have all the loot and gold you can carry, you can make free with their women and tell your grandchildren tall stories," I told him as I tucked the bag away.

In the dim light the French continued to thunder across the battlefield while we shot them down but the intervals grew wider. Just before midnight the French gave up.

Exhausted, parched and hungry we were left with the diminishing cries and moans of those who were not yet dead. Most of us started to doze off leaning on each other.

Toward morning we started to bestir ourselves. It was bitterly cold and a fog had descended upon us. We stayed in position, for we knew not where the French were nor what they were plotting. For ourselves we were reluctant to fight today for it was a Sunday. The good Lord might not like it if we started something off on His day. Later in the day the fog cleared. There before us was the bloody, silent heaps of what had been recently the French army. What was left of it had dissolved, disappeared.

Heavy patrols were sent out and ran into odd parties of French that they chased away.

"Have you heard about that stupid blind man who got himself killed in front of Warwick's men?" said Len in the late evening.

"Blind man? Whatever are you talking about? What would a blind man be doing on a battlefield?" I asked incredulously.

"It is true, some important chap got some knights to lead him so he could have a go at us and we killed the lot."

Rumours like that run around every battlefield. At that point Sir John came by so we asked him if he had heard of it.

"Yes it is true. King John of Bohemia that was."

"Stupid old bastard!" we all said.

With the destruction of the main French army, the King had three options. Link up with the Flemish and make new plans with them, march directly on Paris before the French could recover, or go along the coast to Calais or some such place to establish a proper route of supply and reinforcement from England.

The army was short of men, horses and supplies of all sorts, the only port available at the moment was the little port of Crotoy at the mouth of the Somme. The capture of such a place as Calais would provide a good base on the shortest route to England.

If France was to be conquered and held then a base like Calais was essential. So on the 28th, having buried our dead and looted the enemy dead, we set off jubilantly on a leisurely march through Etaples, Bologne and Wissant to arrive at the west side of Calais. Little did I know that five hundred and seventy years later I would again be a soldier marching through these places.

On our arrival at Calais the French commander shut the gates and a siege began.

Chapter Three

A broad belt of waterlogged countryside surrounded the town – it was autumn – through it meandered the river Hem which entered the sea north of Calais at which point it widened out to form the harbour. There was a double wall around the town and a double ditch, this was backed up by the citadel and several angle towers. To take the town by storm was out of the question at the moment. The marshy ground was unsuitable for heavy catapults or the new guns. A siege it would have to be. At least we had better lines of communication to England now the problem of supplies was solved and there was a trickle of fresh men and horses.

So we camped to the west side of the town, the Flemish army arrived to hold the dunes to the east, and between us the marshy ground to the south was easily blocked.

We were stood looking at the town one morning several days after our arrival and expressing concern to each other about the coming of winter, with us all in tents while the enemy was snug in stone buildings, when we saw movement at the town gate. People were coming through in a column and heading slowly towards us. Soon we could see they were civilians not soldiers. Mainly women and children, with a few old men with them, and also people on crutches or hurdles. They were a ragged, frightened lot, one or two were waving what passed for white flags. We took our stations.

"Oh dear! Now what is this lot in aid of?" said Len.

"It means the enemy are worried about running out of food so they are tipping out all the useless mouths," replied Peter.

"Why should we feed them?" was the general attitude.

There were now several hundred of them and the gate of the town closed behind them.

A knight came riding up.

"Let them through! It is the King's command."

So we waved these people towards us and the knight, who spoke French, led them away. We counted over fifteen hundred of them.

At the King's command they were fed, given some supplies then told to go well away and stay away.

Knowing that we were in for a long siege that would stretch through the winter the King set his carpenters, pioneers and spare men to build a wooden town for his soldiers. It was laid out symmetrically, all roads leading into the centre where a large market square was formed. This town was named New Town in French and was to have two regular market days a week to which the locals were invited to bring their goods and produce for sale. They did so immediately, for Calais, their main market was sealed off and there was no alternative.

At this point we heard about the Scottish invasion of England which ended in tears for them. We not only soundly beat them, we captured their King. It was all well worth a celebration for us.

The siege dragged on with skirmishes and clashes. There were raids into the enemy countryside, some going as far as St Omer. We of Sir John's command did not take part in these raids but we did man the siege lines and skirmish with the enemy and took pot shots at the enemy when the chance presented itself.

The market became popular with our troops and the locals, it also brought a lot of girls out of hiding.

One day I wandered with Len into the market intent on buying some fresh eggs before going on to the new tavern for the evening.

There were two women on a stall that seemed to be in a hurry to close down.

"What's the rush?" I asked in English.

"We don't want to be caught on the road when it gets dark," said the comely-looking, older one who was probably a couple of years older than I.

I laughed, "You are in no danger. You traders are all under the King's protection."

"What good would that be to me if I am way laid by some robber or worse in the dark. I would have my throat cut before your King could raise his hat to me."

We all laughed at the thought of the King raising his hat to a poor French working girl. Len then asked her how she came to speak English so well.

"Ah monsieur my husband would often take me across the Channel when he went there to trade, and before that I had picked up quite a bit at the convent school."

42

"You learnt English at a French convent school?" I asked unbelievingly.

"Yes, but not as part of our schooling. We had a couple of English women with us who were taking the veil."

"And what of your husband?"

"He died some two years ago."

Her companion said little to us as her English was too poor. I could see that Len was interested in the widow so I cut him out quickly.

"If you are worried about being caught on the road at nightfall I'll walk with you. Then you will be safe." That seemed to startle her and she conferred with her friend. Not wanting to let the grass grow under my feet I began to load her hand cart.

"Do you know how far it is to my place?"

"Who cares? If you can walk it, I will have no problem."

Len now turned his attention to the younger woman.

"Fancy an evening stroll, Len?"

"Why not."

In no time at all we dismantled their stall and loaded everything onto the cart, with me pushing and the widow walking beside me we set off.

"What is your name then?"

"Isobel." What a coincidence!

"And you?"

"Tom."

"Do you have a lady friend in England?"

"No."

Now why did I say that? A vision of the other Isobel waiting for me in Huntingdon rose up. Isobel was getting better looking with every stop. It was a long time since I had spoken to a pretty woman. If I had told the truth the friendship would have died on the spot. I had no ulterior motive, I just wanted a respectable female to talk to.

So we chatted as we walked along out of the military town past the guards and into the countryside.

Her husband had caught some disease and was dead in a weekend. They had no children. He had left her a little farm holding with cows, chickens, fruit trees and a vegetable plot which gave her an adequate living with only one mouth to feed. She had lost her family when she was very young and had been brought up by nuns until her husband Phillip had spotted her one day working in the fields. He had been ten years older than she was. She had been glad to escape the nuns and he had been good to her, then in no time at all he was dead. She fell silent for a while.

Len and the other woman, Beatrice, were walking further and further behind us. We now came to a little group of huts where Beatrice lived. We parted company there and Len turned for home, for two is company and three a crowd, and he knew where and when he could see Beatrice again if he wanted to.

By now our talk had become more light-hearted.

She lived about five miles away from the market in a little wooden hut set in isolation in a small garden. Geese squawked at us as we reached the rickety gate.

"Do you live all alone here?"

"Oh yes. I do have friends all around."

It didn't look any worse than the peasant huts back in Papworth.

"Would it be alright if I come out to see you when I am free? I have enjoyed talking to you."

"Well you can always see me in that market place of yours."

"I want more than to push your cart twice a week."

"We shall see," she said with a grin.

I took her hand and kissed it. It was a very small, smooth hand for somebody who worked every daylight hour.

We murmured our goodbyes and something seemed to pass between us.

I set off in the twilight towards camp with my heart beating faster than it had a right to.

A few days later there was a disturbance. The French, counting on our King's mercy, opened the town gate and ejected hundreds more civilians.

This time the King was not feeling noble. We turned them back with shouts and threats. The French didn't want them either.

This crowd of people were trapped without food and water between us and Calais. Dejected and apathetic they sat down in full view of both sides. We hardened our hearts; surely the enemy would not allow their kith and kin to suffer and die right there before them.

Heavy rain that night added to their misery.

It was nearly a week before I saw Isobel again. She seemed pleased to see me. Again I pushed her cart home for her. We chatted happily and this time she invited me to dinner for tomorrow.

I had to seek permission to be out of camp for I might not be back before evening roll call, it was granted with a knowing grin.

My arrival at Isobel's for dinner was not greeted with much joy. I felt something was wrong. She seemed nervous as I entered her home.

We sat together and drank beer while I found it difficult to get her to talk. She was nervous and twitchy. The room was divided by a low partition just like that of Mrs Rodgers.

Then I heard a movement; it was not the movement of a rat.

Had I been lured here for some evil reason?

The French were noted for treachery.

I jumped, brushed Isobel to one side, drew my dagger and went beyond the partition. There appeared to be nobody there, but I had foraged and looted in France long enough to know something was wrong. Isobel now saw the dagger in my hand and beseeched me to leave. I ignored her.

There was a large box in the far corner. I stepped forward in the gloom and flung the lid open. It was full of clothes and things.

There was an almost audible gasp from behind the box.

"Come out this instant!" I shouted in broken French, half expecting some stunted French assassin to emerge.

To my surprise a small trembling boy appeared, all he had in his hand was a crust of bread.

"What the devil is this?"

Isobel now caught my arm. Did she believe I would kill some hungry frightened child? It had been done by others.

"Let him go, don't send him back!" she pleaded, trembling like a leaf.

"Back? Back where? Who is he?"

"Don't harm him he's only a child."

I put my dagger away, which seemed to calm both of them.

"What is this all about?"

"Promise me you won't send him back," pleaded Isobel.

"Who is he and where is he from?"

"He is the son of a friend of mine from Calais."

I then saw the light.

"He is from that group of people that has been ejected from Calais."

She nodded. The boy was petrified; he knew not what we said for we spoke in English.

"How did he get here? None of them are allowed through our lines. It is the King's command."

"He is but a small boy; he got through unseen and came straight to me."

"Well he will have to go straight back again."

"No! No! You can't do that, he will die. He is only a small boy and he can cause your army no harm."

"Are his parents here?"

"No, only him."

"Then you had better feed him and get him out of here. If our patrols find him he is done for."

Isobel was profuse in her thanks. The boy kept his distance and ate ravenously. Isobel filled his pocket with more food and then let him out into the gathering night with whispered instruction of where to go.

She came back to me full of gratitude and I took liberties with her delightful body. Then guilt seized me and I did not go too far.

We talked for a while. The prospect of a meal faded. I decided to go before we went any further. She wanted me to stay but I told her I had duties to perform and could not stay. I wanted to sort my feelings out before I got any deeper with her. We parted with a show of affection.

The following day was terrible. Looking out across the open ground we could see the wretched people huddled together, their dead friends and relatives around them. They no longer had the strength to call for mercy, water or God. They just huddled together and died one by one as a drizzly rain fell on them. For the first time I looked at these people as real people, not just alien figures passing by. I felt better that I had let one of their children escape this fate but it was hard to watch.

It did me more good than I knew to meet Isobel in the market again and to walk back with her through the evening to her house. We chatted quite happily and I graduated to a good night kiss.

Len it was who queried how it was that Isobel, whose other name was Jaifrok, came to be fair in a land of swarthy people. Her carriage also was not of a peasant girl. Perhaps, he suggested, her real father had been an English seadog. I did not worry about such things. One day in March I walked her home from the market and when we reached her house a thunderstorm broke out. I stayed in out of the weather and we ate and talked. We held hands and embraced. It was too much to resist: we ended up in the straw. She was naked and eager as I. She had a beautiful body. When we made love it was like nothing that had gone before. Our passion swept us onto a higher mind-blowing plane. We could not let each other go until a cock crowed somewhere.

It was with difficulty that we let each other go. I got dressed and away just as daylight streaked the sky.

This was no wartime fling: this was a love like I had never known even with my wife now in Huntingdon.

From then on two nights a week after the market I slept with Isobel. The guilt about the wife in England, or the chaplain ranting on about the penalty for adultery, faded away each time I took her in my arms.

The lance covered for my absence and passed bawdy remarks, though even a fool must have known this was no ordinary liaison. I was in any case not the only one in the English army besieging Calais that had a French lady friend. As long as we carried out our duties nothing was said. Things, however, were said about the girls, some quite young, that gathered in and around the tavern. Where else would girls find food and fun in this ravaged land? Sometimes the authority would move them on but with a host of sex-starved men and lonely, hungry women they were on a loser.

In the spring rumours went around that the French were planning to relieve Calais and an army was gathering around Arras under their self-styled King Phillip. These preparations went on through the spring and into the summer.

In April we watched helplessly as blockade runners by the dozen sailed into Calais. Where were our ships? If the enemy could keep that up the siege was a waste of time and effort.

In response to this our King had a fort built at Ryesbank to block the harbour entrance with heavy cannon. He also increased the strength of the fleet and put in charge such people as the Earl of Northampton who would carry the war to the enemy ships.

By this time Isobel and I were spending three nights a week together. The inevitable question arose.

"What shall we do when the siege comes to an end and I have to go away?" It left my heart cold but had to be faced. The reply was astonishing.

"It matters not, for a more important terrible thing is about to befall us all."

"How can you say such a thing!"

"It is foretold that shortly there will be a disaster for the human race. Be not afraid, if we perish we shall return."

She was a witch!!!

"I shall love you in the next life and beyond."

What was she talking about? What did it mean? In the next life and beyond? Everyone knew that after death you would be consigned to Heaven or Hell according to your merits. Beyond?

I now stiffened up and pulled away from her.

"What you say is heresy."

"It is the truth as you will see."

I was now more than apprehensive. To go on listening to her could bring all sorts of trouble. Morning was in any case breaking and I made haste to leave her and return to camp. Terrible strange thoughts bore in on me.

For the next two days I was in torment. If Isobel Jaifrok was a witch and a sorceress I must denounce her or put my immortal soul in peril.

I went to the priest to seek his advice but my courage or whatever failed me – witches were sure to be burnt alive when caught – so I confessed to adultery instead. His condemnation fell on deaf ears. If Isobel Jaifrok was an agent of the devil she already had my soul in her hand.

I missed one planned meeting with her but could not go on. My comrades noticed my strange behaviour.

"He's bewitched," declared Len.

I rounded on him for he had touched a sore point. Words flew and we squared up to each other. Never before had this happened. We were comrades, we had stood by each other in adversity and danger, had shared the good things that came our way. Now here I was willing to strike him and cause him hurt. Peter had to come between us until I cooled down. I turned on my heels and left the billet to seek consolation in the tavern. That was no use so I went for a walk along our perimeter facing the enemy. I cared not what they did.

The following day I apologised to Len for my conduct and he in turn apologised for upsetting me though he knew not what it was. The general consensus was that I was in love. How true.

When I met Isobel again she behaved as though nothing strange had been said. I walked her home as usual and she set me on fire again, asking me to stay the night. How could I say no? Once we were settled in for the night, I resumed where we left off last time I was there.

"What did you mean the other day when you spoke of death and beyond and the disaster that is about to befall us all? Who told you all this?" Perhaps she was the innocent victim of some evil sorcerer.

"Nobody has told me anything. I found out by sitting here all alone thinking about the meaning of life and what is ahead for all of us."

So she had been sitting here all alone through the long nights letting her imagination run wild. That was better than being a witch.

"Well you forget it all now. Nobody can foretell the future. It is all in God's hands."

"Yes we can and I can prove it."

"Alright then tell me when Calais will fall to us?"

"August."

Now I had something to measure her by. Then she added:

"You will leave France in January."

"We will see."

"When is this disaster to hit the human race?" I asked.

"It will start next year." There was a pause as we stood close looking at each other.

"Now will you stay to dinner tonight and keep me company. If I am wrong in these things you will know soon enough."

How was I to refuse even though my mind was in a turmoil?

I tried to forget the things she had said, and over the next few weeks neither of us mentioned such things. Life was too short and I loved her. If she was going to Hell, I wanted to go with her. The priest said I would anyway.

Spring turned to summer and we were happy together; may the siege last forever.

In July the French relief force around Arras began to move. A new campaign season was upon us.

The French approached Calais from the east but the Flemish would not let them pass, so they moved round to the west and got themselves into an awkward position. Isobel Jaifrok now passed behind enemy lines, but not for long.

The French were unwilling to fight at a disadvantage. After three days of parley they crept away in the night.

The garrison of Calais – faced with starvation having eaten all their horses, dogs, cats and rats – were shattered by the failure of the relief force. Though several thousand strong, the relief force had refused combat and gone away. There was only one thing left for the garrison to do. Surrender!

It was August.

King Edward sent food into the city immediately, then got rid of all those that still appeared to favour the French king. Calais was henceforth to be an English port and space was needed inside the city for English settlers.

A truce was signed between the two nations to last until 26th of June next year.

In 1346–7 we English had won a series of victories, not only at Crecy; we had overrun Poitou, captured Calais and conquered Scotland putting an English nominee on its throne. Everywhere one looked, English arms had been victorious.

"Do you believe me now?" asked Isobel.

"So what now is to become of you and I?"

"You will go home to your wife and I shall have your child to remind me of you."

I stood still for a moment with my mouth open.

"How did you know I was married? What is this about a child? When?"

"I have known for some time that you are married. The child is due in January, the month you will leave France. I shall call it Simon after you."

"I cannot leave you Isobel. I love you."

"You must and you will. Come now let us eat."

She was taking things so calmly. It was only after we had eaten that the conversation resumed.

"Who told you I was married?"

"Nobody. I know you have a wife and son in England and you must leave me for them. It makes no difference. I love you. Your wife and I will both have a son of yours."

"You could not know unless somebody told you."

"That is not so. I can look back into the past as well as the future. You will go back to your family where you belong, but I will always love you."

"How do you know all this unless you are a witch?" I was full of foreboding.

She laughed. "Do I look like a witch? Come let us rest awhile. Before you go home I shall show you how to look into the past and the future. Till then let us forget the world." With that she stood up and took my hand.

So we went to her bed, embraced each other and made love through into the early hours of a warm August day. My mind still was in turmoil and our passion as a result was not as strong as usual.

With the departure of the King in September for a triumphal parade in London more people were agitating to get off home. Those of us under Sir John were selected to form the rear guard, others would be staying as the garrison. I tried to get myself transferred to that garrison.

"We might be able to stay together always," I told Isobel. "I have applied to be transferred to the garrison."

"No," she replied. "They will not let you stay. If you did it would complicate matters, for your wife would want to join you."

As always she was right.

As autumn came on there was much movement round Calais. A rough demarcation line was drawn and Isobel was on the wrong side of it! I could not openly go into the French area for if they caught me they would execute me as a spy. If the English caught me they would execute me as a deserter. The thought of deserting did come to me, I would hide away permanently with Isobel. I dismissed the idea, I was bound to get caught, I didn't look or sound French.

How could I get a message to her. There was nobody I could trust and they would face the same risks as I.

Was this the end of the affair?

Then our commanders decided that the local traders should be allowed into the town with their goods. Calais was too small to supply all its own food and with the weather worsening supplies from England were sure to be disrupted.

So the traders came back. The French were in favour of the idea as they needed the Calais trade more than we did.

I watched for Isobel and at last I found her. She had gone to the smaller market in the new town, which was rapidly declining, because that is where we met. She was with Beatrice.

We were both excited at finding each other again. How could I let her go?

"My request to stay with the garrison has been refused," I told her sadly.

"I know." she said and laid her head on my shoulder. We were silent for a while. What now?

"I see that most of the new town is empty, there must be a spare billet for us tonight." My heart leapt at the suggestion. Another night with this lovely woman lifted my spirits.

"I'll see what I can find."

I went off to spy out a suitable hideaway while Isobel had a quiet word with Beatrice. So it came about. Beatrice was escorted to the demarcation line by Len while Isobel and I slid off to an abandoned gentleman's lodging.

I had to accept the inevitable: we could not be together much longer. We made love long into the night as if there was no tomorrow.

She agreed to stay in the new town until the next market day then she would go off home with Beatrice.

"Are you a sorceress?" I asked her once again.

"No! No! Perhaps next time I come I will show you how I can tell about the past and the future. I will bring my pendulum with me."

"Pendulum?"

"Yes my pendulum tells what I want to know."

"You are joking."

"No, next time I come I will bring my pendulum and answer any question you have."

"Any question?"

"Yes."

Too soon it was market day again; Beatrice returned and Isobel went off with her. For the best part of a week I racked my brains for a question she could not know the answer to.

Next time Isobel and Beatrice came into Calais itself, where there was more trade. I chatted with her most of the day, then when she was less busy I asked her if she still wanted to try her pendulum on me.

"Oh yes. Let us go over to that place in new town; you give me the questions and I shall get the pendulum to give me the answers."

So we left Beatrice in charge of the stall while we walked over into the new town to the lodgings we had used before. She then asked me for the questions.

"Name my son, my father and the woman my wife is lodging with in Huntingdon."

"Very well, you stay out here and I'll be back with my answers, but I already know your son is named John."

She left me there speechless as she went into the hut. Perhaps without knowing it I had let the name slip or one of my friends had told her. I did not have long to wait before she came back.

"Your father's name is Joseph and your wife is lodging with Mrs Rodgers.

I stared at her in disbelief.

"How could you know unless you got it from one of my friends?"

"My pendulum told me."

"Let me see this pendulum."

She pulled out a little wooden box and opened it. There inside was a silver pendant.

"Now do you believe me?"

"No."

I walked back to the stall with her. How had she known? She would say it was no more than the pendulum.

I could not go home with her for that night or to our little nest in New Town for I was on duty with Sir Harold. In fact it was the last I saw of her before embarkation. Sir Harold who was aware of our relationship made sure I was on unavoidable duty every market day.

We never said goodbye before I left France in January 1348.

I heard from Len via Beatrice that Isobel had given birth to a son just before we sailed, again like she said she would.

Chapter Four

We landed at Dover and proceeded at a sedate pace through Kent, there was no point in wearing out our horses or infantry.

We arrived at London and we were all feted and feasted, the Lord Mayor and others gave speeches and the beer flowed like a river. I got the impression that some people felt they had waved at enough returning soldiers since September. Nevertheless as intended we stayed in London for a while and enjoyed ourselves.

The weather was getting bad and many were in favour of staying in London until the weather changed. The married men and those with ladies waiting for them were all for pressing on. In the Huntingdon contingent the married men were out-voted. So we tarried in London while the winter weather got worse to the north, or so we were told.

There was much jollity for not only had we survived a war but we had come back with a lot more money and loot than many people had seen. Conmen and women closed in on us.

Len, Peter, John and myself stayed together; we wished to hang on to our hard gotten gains unless a reasonable price was offered. We drank with the rest but felt safer together, for London was notorious for all sorts of shady people. Others not so bright were being slowly fleeced. We were lucky also with our billet; we, with one or two others, were in a little inn owned by an ex-soldier. He put us wise to many of the antics of avaricious civilians.

The fleshpots of London soon became tiresome to men of our like. A dozen of us with Sir Harold decided to press on home regardless of the weather reports; we were not happy just hanging about avoiding trouble.

So with Sir Harold leading we set off and on the first day despite the weather reached Waltham Abbey and there stopped for two nights. The next leg of our journey took us to Ware. It was freezing cold with heavy snow almost blocking our way. On the fifth day we pressed on to Buntingford. We lodged at a small abbey there which seemed to have little food left for us.

I had felt a little guilty at having left John behind but by now it was clear he would have never made it this far.

On the eighth day eight of us pressed on, the others stayed because they or their horses needed a longer rest. It was hinted though never said that we were too much of a burden, not wishing to out stay our welcome we moved on. Sir Harold said we would be better off at Royston where a friend of his lived.

It was a dreadful journey to make in midwinter. Perhaps those in London who advised us to wait a month were right. The road was so bad that we had to lead our horses much of the way. In places it almost disappeared.

"We'll be alright if we don't stray, this is an old Roman road," said Sir Harold.

"No wonder the Romans went home then," replied Len.

But Sir Harold seemed to know where he was going and led us to the Manor at Royston of Sir Martin Jollie. He willingly took us in.

There was a roaring fire and lots of hot food as well as a dry clean place for us to sleep. Sir Martin had also been at Crecy so we had much to talk about.

We stayed for several days, Sir Martin said if ever things got too hard we would be welcome to serve with him, but we were only concerned to get home.

The weather showed improvement and with Papworth only fourteen miles away we set off. Surely we could make it in one day, after all we were supposed to be hardened soldiers.

"Those with further to go than Papworth can stay a while at my manor," said Sir Harold.

I would stop at my father's place before going on to Huntingdon.

So we pressed forward on the last stage across the terrible roads and cut by an icy wind. At Caxton Gibbet we passed a dead criminal frozen solid.

We got spread out as we approached Papworth; in the gathering gloom only three of us were together.

It took a lot of banging on my father's door, and loud questions from inside which I was too cold to answer, before it was opened.

As soon as he saw it was me, father grabbed me in his arms; his only son had returned! He dragged me to the fire, bellowing orders. Everyone appeared from the gloom of that rat-infested hovel to slap me on the back, shake my hand or kiss me. I was home.

On my insistence, that night I slept in the smithy with the two horses, just like the old days: I would never get any sleep otherwise. I slept as though dead.

I awoke late next morning. I could hear people moving about and talking in low voices in the house as I lay there thinking of all the things that had happened to me since I last lay here. After Isobel Jaifrok, would my life with my wife get back to normal?

I got up and had a good breakfast. A thaw was beginning. Mrs Ingram came along to find out where her son John was and was he alright? She brightened up when I assured her he was fine. Somebody had been despatched to Huntingdon to inform my wife I was on my way.

Father was as happy as a sand boy.

"Now the war is over you and your family can come back to your own house." He was bubbling with joy. I did not have the courage to tell him the war was not over and if it was I had no intention of toiling my life away in the smithy.

I set off on the last seven miles to see my wife and son.

As I rode across the stone bridge at Huntingdon I saw Isobel waiting for me, as soon as she recognised me she came running. I jumped off my horse as I reached her and we flung ourselves into each others arms.

Isobel Jaifrok was gone.

We walked together along the road to our lodging and John came running out, he was over three years of age. I picked him up and hugged him tight. This was where I belonged; the other Isobel was just a wartime fling after all.

Or was she?

After a couple of nights with Mrs Rodgers I decided I would to back to Papworth. There was no privacy here, not enough room and no sound barrier between us and Mrs Rodgers which made it embarrassing when Isobel and I cuddled up at night. There was also the fact that I was still employed by Sir Harold. He was in Papworth and we had our house there next to the smithy, all of which was true. I felt I had sufficient standing now to deal with father and once the truce was over in June the war would begin again and there was no way I could avoid that.

So we moved back to our house in Papworth, cleaned it up and settled in nice and snug. John loved being near his granddad and

Judith and they loved him being there which gave us plenty of opportunity to get Isobel pregnant again.

I went up to the Manor House to see Sir Harold; he had arrears of pay for me which came in handy though I was not short of cash yet. We stopped to talk for a while.

"Are you game for another expedition in the summer, Tom?"

"I don't see why not, I am still in your lance, sir, unless you want to get rid of me."

"Grief no! You were all excellent soldiers and good company but in your case you have a young son to worry about now, I thought you might have second thoughts."

"He's got this far without harm, one summer campaign will not be as long and I would like to see Paris and be in at the final."

"So you shall. As you say one quick campaign and it should all be over, I shall see Sir John when the time is ripe and we shall see. The sooner the better."

Two weeks later John Ingram turned up and was welcomed by all.

"Well John will you be with us on the next expedition?"

"I don't think so. All that marching about and living rough, I think I will get me a job in Huntingdon, find myself a young woman and settle down. I have seen all I want to see of France."

"Well good luck to you, but there is not much work in Huntingdon these days. In fact the whole area seems to be stagnating."

Isobel and I talked about my future. She was not in favour of me going off again for another two years. I pointed out the next campaign should be shorter and I was committed to serve Sir Harold. If I ended my commitment, how would I earn a living? The smithy would not support two families and she knew what I thought about being a blacksmith for life. Another point was that if the war was resumed there was not much chance of experienced people like me avoiding impressments, this time it should be a short campaign, then peace ever after.

We could only live for each day. I did odd jobs for father, spent time at the Manor House and rolled in the hay with Isobel. War seemed a long way off.

Slowly spring crept up on us and Sir Harold wanted to see more of me and all the others of his lance and men at arms. It was time to toughen up and prepare for the resumption of the war.

The spring shaded into summer and instead of resumption of the war there was an extension of the armistice. This did not stop minor fighting in Brittany and Gascony. Sir John apparently saw not much profit and honour in those places and was waiting for a major expedition under the King.

In the meantime Isobel got bigger.

A rumour was rife that France and Italy could not fight because God had smitten them with a terrible plague. That made me think of Isobel Jaifrok; could this be her prophesy coming true? It should be no problem for us, we were an island and God was on our side.

Under pressure from father, I gave a hand in the smithy from time to time but I was glad when we set off again for a week at the Great Annual Fair at Huntingdon, where I could once more compete in the archery contests, watch the jousting tournaments and chat with old comrades.

In the evening round the camp fire or in the taverns I found the main topic of conversation was not past present or future tournaments and wars, but the plague upon the Continent. Everyone now thought that it would spread to England because of the coming and going of traders.

With the contests over, in which again I came third, I rode back to Papworth.

Then one day we heard the bad news, the plague had indeed arrived in England. It was in a place many miles away called Melcome Regis. That was better than London we all said, it could be contained in the west. Not that anybody said how.

Week by week it advanced towards us.

Father was taken ill and shortly died, something to do with his lungs.

Who was now to run the smithy? I agreed to take on the job part time until I was called for service with Sir Harold. I was still required to attend the manor farm from time to time. One of my brother-in-law also came along from time to time.

The growing threat of the plague was causing concern and agitation and I found myself with the Squire, priest, constable and one or two others trying to calm people down.

To avert the advancing evil we joined in prayer Sundays, Wednesdays and Fridays. There was a marked growth in confessions and penance. Still the pestilence was reported at places ever nearer.

Those who were most worried went barefoot in procession around the church. We were informed again and again by the clergy that pestilence and early death was quite often the result of sin. Heal souls that had gone astray and the plague would die away. Which did not explain why innocent babies were dying.

"Sin or not it will probably die away in the winter," said Sir Harold. "Most of the tales are a gross exaggeration."

"Exaggerations to frighten people with lurid tales is to the advantage of the clergy," said some. Others had a deeper criticism which in some countries could have led them to the stake if voiced aloud. "If God is so good and powerful why is he doing this? Either he is not good or he is not powerful enough to protect his people." At this stage nobody questioned if there was a God.

In fear of our lives we went to church more than ever and listened to rumours from afar.

Autumn came and then winter and no plague had reached us. It spread itself across the Midlands and struck London and still we remained untouched. Perhaps it would burn itself out before it reached us. Perhaps after all God would protect this area of the land.

While this was agitating all minds, Isobel gave birth to a daughter, Kathleen. Then she quickly fell pregnant again to our surprise.

The armistice with France was extended again, for both sides were running short of fit young men and revenues were down. The plague was said to be more virulent on the Continent which was God's will. I now often thought of Isobel Jaifrok and her prophesy.

Winter gave way to spring and still we were untouched. Optimism began to grow and increasingly we felt we had been spared, after all we were God fearing people.

Then it happened.

It was Huntingdon. People fled from there, some coming to Papworth. We turned away all who were not relatives; we did not want their problems. We soldiers now became guardians of the approach roads. We insisted travellers keep travelling: there was no room in our village. Some did not even want close relatives in. The talk of Christian charity gave way to self-preservation. We closed ourselves off. It was too late!

A parish meeting had been called to decide how we could increase our vigilance and organise our manpower to protect us, and should we make travellers go round rather than through the village. The priest also wanted to tell us how we could appeal more earnestly to God and the Saints to protect us from this terrible threat.

As we gathered to enter the vestry we saw approaching one of the villagers in what appeared to be an inebriated state. He wobbled along the street and had trouble getting through the church gate.

"That's all we need, a drunken disruption," I said.

"Don't worry, I will not let him enter the vestry," said Sir Harold.

He and I stood watching the approach of the wobbly figure whom I now recognised, the rest were moving into the vestry. He came closer as we barred his way; he was not known for over drinking but things were different now everyone was feeling the stress. He would be no problem, he was not strong and robust and in his condition should be easy to deal with – one small push and he would fall down.

He saved us the trouble: he collapsed at our feet.

"Leave him there until after the meeting," said Sir Harold.

As we turned to follow the others into the vestry one of the Huntingdon migrants who had been stood watching at the door pushed past us and bent over the figure on the ground peering into his face. Then he began pulling the tunic off him.

"What do you think you are doing?" demanded Sir Harold. These town people would take anything if not stopped. The man on the ground was now gasping for breath, his eyes were rolling and his face was blotchy, he was trembling like a leaf. It now occurred to us he might not be drunk but ill.

The migrant bared the man's upper body, raised an arm and pointed at the man's armpit. Boils!

We knew instantly from the tales we had heard what that meant. The boils seemed to grow before our eyes surrounded by red blotches.

Sir Harold and I looked at each other in consternation. He was the first to recover his wits. He went into the vestry and in a loud voice ordered everyone to go home and stay there until further notice. Once they knew the reason, there was no stopping them. The victim was left where he fell.

I told Isobel what had happened as soon as I got home. Perhaps I told her too abruptly or she was too full of fear and dread. Whatever.

She went into screaming hysterics, I had a desperate job with her and she set the two children off as well. The place was like a mad house. Judith rushed in to see what the noise was all about. Isobel grabbed hold of her and kept screaming.

"The plague! The plague!"

Judith managed after a struggle to get a better control of the situation.

Then Isobel collapsed and went into premature labour.

I managed to calm the two children down and take them into father's house. As I went Judith whispered.

"Is it true?"

"Yes," I said hoarsely.

Judith blanched then turned her attention back to Isobel who had started screaming again.

If I thought this was a terrible day, worse was to come as we all knew.

The premature baby was undersize and not fully formed; in fact he looked as though he had only just survived and he looked ugly to me. We had already decided to call him Norman.

With his birth things seem to quieten.

We could not take the baby to be christened and as he didn't look as though he would survive long I went to the priest and persuaded him to come and christen our poor child at home. The priest took some persuading even to open the door. With my pleading he relented and came with me. If he went just to my house and straight back he could hardly come to harm.

Now Norman was christened and the door barred, we settled down to see this thing through with some hope of avoidance as long as we stayed put. Or so we thought. Within days Judith was taken ill and the plague was confirmed. She lingered for four days in pain and distress. She was tended by one of her daughters; she gave off the most dreadful smell. We were grateful that the priest risked his life to give her absolution.

I went to help dig her grave, for the sooner the body was disposed of the better. Then once more the doors were barred and we were isolated waiting to see who would be next.

Each morning we would search each other's armpits for telltale signs.

The foul air in our hut got too much and one morning I ventured out into sweet, refreshing morning air.

All was silent and still. I walked through the village and saw nobody. I was tempted to call out but desisted. I walked up to the Manor House and banged on the door. After several knockings Sir Harold himself from inside called out.

"Who is it and what do you want?"

"It is I, Thomas Simon, sir. Is all well with you and yours?"

"Are you mad? Get back to your family and stay there until someone in authority tells you otherwise!"

I wandered back into the village. There was still no movement or sound. It was all very eerie and strange. I had no mind for all this despair, I decided to go home and kill a chicken for dinner.

On the way I decided to call out at each house I passed and break the silence by enquiring about their welfare.

Some did not answer, some told me to go away, some said all was well so far but did not emerge.

At the constable's house I was greeted with cries of anguish and calls for help. I had none to give.

We could not stay in our huts forever. The animals had to be tended, food got in.

After a good dinner I persuaded Isobel and the children to come and sit outside in the fresh air. We could come to no harm if we did not come into contact with anybody. If we were going to get the plague we should have got it from Judith by now.

So we sat outside and the two elder children began to play and laugh and chatter. That brought others out of their stinking hovels, but we all stayed clear while we congratulated each other. Eventually the constable came out and sat down. He was white faced and had been crying, he was all a tremble. We learnt that all his children and his wife were infected and were in the last stages; he did not expect them to see the day through.

Somebody went to fetch the priest and reluctantly he entered the constable's house to give absolution. He was braver than most. But we knew sooner or later we would have to bring bodies out.

Before many days more families were stricken. Try as we might we could not avoid all contact with each other. The dead had to be buried, orphans taken care of. Every day was a nightmare.

Then one terrible morning, after Isobel had spent a restless night, they were there. Small boils and red blotches under her arms and in her crutch.

A fearful coldness came upon me.

I resolved to stay with her to the end: I could do no other. I went for the priest but it was too late; he was down with a fever. Later a curate came and gave Isobel absolution. Nobody had been known to survive once the plague got them. The curate allocated a plot for my dear wife outside the churchyard. I would have to dig the grave myself for the sexton was not well.

When I returned I found our dear daughter Kathleen crying and showing the first signs of the plague. Surely God was not so cruel as to infect such an innocent child. Isobel was soon delirious and in great pain, the boils were terrible to behold. Molly took John and the baby while I stayed with Isobel and Kathleen day and night. The stench was terrible and the sight of my wife and daughter dying slowly before my eyes nearly drove me mad.

I was thankful when Isobel passed away soon to be followed by Kathleen.

The next few days passed in a haze I knew not how I got through. I buried them together in the same grave. I was afraid it would be my turn before the task was done.

Instead on my return Molly handed me the baby and pointed out the ominous signs. Never was a day like this. What sins had we committed to suffer like this? Why did the clergy insist that God was a loving deity?

My baby died rather quickly for he was not very strong. There was only John, my three year old son and I left. Molly also survived. We could not understand why. Nobody and nothing was the same again.

How had Isobel Jaifrok known that this was to befall us. I did not believe that she was in league with the devil who had caused it.

In the following month Sir Harold was infected and died so we had a new squire, his younger brother. Like everyone else Sir Harold was buried quickly.

I went to the Manor House soon after with Len Roper to see how we stood with the new squire.

He told us bluntly that he had no use for fighting men, if pressed he would pay scutage and attend his lands, he was not even interested in the Knighthood. If we liked we could work for him on the land at three pence a day, he was short of labour because of the plague.

We declined and our income disappeared.

No mention was made of the horse and other things acquired in his brother's service so I kept them. He said he could not afford the small amount of arrears owed us. Times were hard he said.

My sister Kathleen, now a widow, came to live with me and John which made things a bit easier.

I still had some money left over from the war and I now had some work in the smithy, but even that was in decline.

By late autumn the plague had moved on and we could take stock. Something like forty per cent of the village had died in the space of four months. Happiness and laughter had died with them.

The price of food in the towns went up for a while because so many fields had not been harvested. The price of labour was up because of the shortage of workers. The prestige of the Church had suffered a severe blow; many of the new village priests were not up to the standard of those lost.

The worst effect was the loss of key family members and the disruption it caused. In some cases, whole families had perished and neighbours had to enter the stinking abodes to remove the bodies. Other bodies were laying around the village but were left to rot into the ground because they did not belong to our community.

A deep depression and fatalism settled upon us.

Winter of 1349–50 was a dismal affair all across the land. Only in the spring did things appear to pick up. There would be less farmland in cultivation but there were less people to feed.

I did odd jobs at the smithy but life seemed to have no meaning anymore.

Then Len Roper turned up to tell me something.

"Remember Sir Martin Jollie at Royston?"

"Yes. Why?"

"Well he is looking for trained soldiers to serve in the Brittany campaign."

"Brittany campaign? There is supposed to be an armistice."

"Maybe so but there has been bickering there all the time and Sir Martin thinks it is going to hot up soon."

"Well I don't know where either side is going to get enough soldiers after last year's plague."

"It will not be a full campaign like the Crecy do, only a fight for Brittany."

Then he came to the point.

"I was thinking of riding down to Royston to see what is on offer. Want to come?"

I did some quick thinking. I was not going to make much of a living in the smithy, my heart was not in it. If I could persuade my sister to take care of John, she had a job at the Manor and a vegetable garden, I could add to her income without having to be fed. Blood stirred within me. The other thing that stirred me was news of a recent defeat for us near Calais and raids by the French on our southern coast. Such insults should not be endured.

"When are you thinking of going?"

"Day after tomorrow."

"Come and see me tomorrow and I'll let you know."

So that night I spoke to my sister and told her. To my surprise she raised no objections, she could manage quite well on the Manor income, odd farm jobs and the bit of land she had. Why should she stand in my way? Soldiering was what I did best. I said she could have my little house alongside the smithy for life and not just while I was away. She would be quite happy and have a chance like me to get her life moving again. I thought she had a man in mind to share it with.

So with Len I rode down to Royston, Peter had died in the plague. Sir Martin was willing to see us. He was full of enthusiasm to put the French back in their place. The threat to Brittany was growing, the commander there, Sir Thomas Dagwood, had been killed in a French ambush. The new commander was beseeching the King for more men but there were hardly any available. We had been beaten outside Calais, our allies were under pressure from the French King in Poitiers, and his armies building up round our possessions in Gascony. If that was not enough French and Spanish ships were running amok in the Channel and boasting they would soon land armies in England. Our King was going to need all the soldiers he could get.

Sir Martin talked of the urgent need for trained men, he talked of Crecy, he talked of the loot we had won last time let alone the glory and the honour. Len and I said little, we didn't need to. Eventually Sir Martin made us an offer, it was similar to that of 1345. Then I had a pregnant wife, now I was single. I was a recruit then and a veteran now, at both times I was unwilling to work my life away at the smithy or some such place, it was soldiering I wanted.

So it was agreed, Len and I would wear livery again and be properly dressed and armed. I would keep my faithful horse; he was still up to it. We were to move into a little hut near the manor and be paid seven pence a day; three of us mounted archers of Sir Martin's lance. It was like coming home again. The third man was Ivan Lane, he was a bit younger than us but had served awhile in Gascony; he seemed a good archer and comrade.

I rode back to Papworth to collect other things I needed and to say goodbye to my son and family and all the others who had survived the plague. I took father's horse with me as a pack horse. Kathleen had no need of him. With everything attended to I hugged my five year old son, told him I would see him again soon, then with Len I rode out of Papworth once more in search of war.

The campaign season was well advanced so Sir Martin concentrated on recruiting and training for next year despite all that chat about getting to Brittany as soon as possible. We did not doubt he was doing the right thing.

In the meantime came news of a spectacular victory for us in the Channel off the town of Winchelsea. The English Channel was English again.

For me it was more than a happy time again of riding, archery, and combat training for in Royston I met Kathleen Topliss, daughter of a dealer in hides. She was quite a well-built woman with flaxen hair, a ready smile, above normal sense and feeling. She was nineteen I was twenty-six. We spent many happy hours together.

On March 10th 1351 we were married. Sir Martin was not too keen but gave us separate accommodation and employed Kathleen in his kitchen. I brought my son down to join us after Easter. From time to time I wondered how my French son, Simon, was getting on. Did he and Isobel Jaifrok survive the plague?

By the summer Kathleen was pregnant.

Sir Martin relied on us veterans to train and discipline the new soldiers, fortunately they were a willing lot, but in the view of Len and I the standard was not as high by comparison with the men of 1346. There were no impressed men which made life easier.

To our surprise we went off to Brittany in the late autumn. We had no great men with us like Warwick or Northampton, let alone a Royal. We were not an expedition but reinforcements. Nevertheless we had confidence in our commanders and we knew we were more than a match for the French.

Chapter Five

We marched through Brittany to the great fortress of Fourges which had recently been captured from the French. Here we joined the garrison under Sir Robert Knollys and awaited on events. The march had been without incident and the civilians seemed well disposed to us.

Rumour said that the French King himself was on his way to deal with us. This did not seem to worry our Breton allies and certainly not us English. But the weeks rolled by and nothing happened.

Len, like many more of our comrades, struck up a friendship with a local woman and on occasion I stood in for him when he was nominated to duty so that he could get away with his lady friend.

"I am getting bored with being cooped up in a castle," I said one day. "I was hoping for a mobile campaign, lots of action, looting and riding."

"You speak for yourself," replied Len. "We're alright here and I'm getting a good ride twice a week." That made us laugh and pass bawdy comments.

To while away the time I put my little command through its paces and kept them toned up: sooner or later there would be action.

Then the French King really did appear and we were besieged. We held them off without too much trouble until Sir William Bentley arrived and the French left. The enemy was unwilling to engage our army in a full-scale battle.

Soon after that we left Fourges and marched about rather aimlessly in the open. This was more to my liking for I had become stale with lack of movement and was getting homesick.

There was much preparation to be done before the enemy came back again as he must.

"I didn't come to France to be a labourer," complained Len. He was missing his lady friend.

"Hard work never hurt anyone," I told him.

67

"That's a load of rubbish as every worker knows. You can easily get a rupture, injure your back or break a leg working. If you believe otherwise you might as well have stayed a village blacksmith."

"I came out here to look after you, what else!"

"Well you are not doing a very good job of it with all this heavy work going on."

We were soon in the field with Sir Robert Knollys getting ready for a clash of arms. Len and I each had some thirty archers under our command though we were still in the lance of Sir Martin.

Our army now gathered at a place called Ploermel which was better than being spread out and liable to being picked off by the French who were now advancing again.

The enemy captured Rennes, the capital of Brittany, some thirty miles away. Both armies were trying to cut across their enemy's line of communication. We marched north on the 14th August, twelve miles on we passed through the village of Mauron and immediately found the enemy coming towards us in great force.

Sir William quickly selected a defensive position on high ground north west of the village. There were only three thousand of us and many were not English but Bretons. The position we took up was not ideal but we had not time to seek a better one. My unit was on the right. The spur of high ground was a little too long for our numbers but nevertheless we stood our ground as directed and watched as the much larger force of the enemy gathered in front of us.

"I think they are trying to frighten us, showing all their numbers," said Len.

"Well they frighten me," said one of our men.

"Just hold your place and listen for my commands and there will be no problems," I assured him.

"These frogs can be very obliging at times," Len told his men.

In front of us hundreds of bees were humming away collecting honey; we hoped soon to change that sound to the humming of our arrows.

Then when they thought all was ready the enemy sent a herald forwards to us.

"Well they have learnt something from Crecy, they don't just charge down on us all higgledy-piggledy," I said.

"Shows they are not very sure, just standing there looking at us," said Len to his troop.

The herald did not stay too long. We had apparently been offered the chance to withdraw quietly, which made some of us laugh.

At the hour of Vespers the enemy began to advance all along their line. Because of the configuration and length of the front our archers could not cover the whole line. As the enemy advanced into range suddenly to my consternation everything seemed to go wrong. Enemy cavalry skilfully using the ground emerged much too close and thundered towards our wedge. They were too close for us to halt them. They struck us and our line broke, some of our men ran away. The men at arms on our left without the support of archers fell back under pressure.

Defeat stared us in the face.

I screamed myself hoarse trying to keep my little group together and facing the enemy. This was the moment when discipline and training is put to the test. I was soaking wet with the heat and with fear as giant horses came at us from yards away.

Some three hundred yards behind us was a line of trees. It slowed the enemy and gave us time to recover. Our left wing had done well and seen the enemy off but our commander Sir William Bentley had been severely wounded.

"Right that is far enough!" I yelled at my men as I got them back in order. "You will win this fight or die right here!!" To emphasise the point I drew my dagger.

It was a very confused fight in that line of trees but we held them while our comrades poured volleys of arrows into the enemy flank. Apparently a large number of the enemy out on our left flank came to a halt at the foot of the slope from heat exhaustion and were shot down in heaps. It was hot enough to us but inside armour it became impossible for them to go on. The enemy commander was killed and at this point their army disintegrated and fled.

The French had been beaten again as at Crecy.

We on the right had not been happy with how the battle started and Sir William had also been startled at the temporary collapse. Though in pain from his wounds he called together subordinate commanders to find the reason why. The finger of guilt was pointed at a mixed group of Breton and English archers. Sir William berated junior commanders for not getting their units more integrated and disciplined, but Breton archers were nowhere near our standard. Many harsh words were said.

After sleeping on it, Sir William decided to make an example of some so that others would stand firm next time.

Thirty archers were to be selected for public execution.

When it came to which thirty he met opposition. So Sir William told us sergeants to pick people out.

I flatly refused.

"None of my men ran away. We only fell back when the line was broken. I will not pick anyone out for such punishment! They did very well when the line was reformed. No I will not pick anyone!"

"It is an order from Sir William. You will do as you are told!" Sir Martin said sternly. Then he added, "You don't have to pick anyone in your own troop."

"I was too busy with my troop to watch others so I am not qualified to point the finger. The French were clever and caught us on the hop but we beat them. Let us leave it at that?"

"We cannot leave it like that. Sir William wants to make an example of somebody."

"Well I am not going to get involved and none of my troop will be selected." At this point Len joined his objections to mine. With that we both turned and walked away. We were short enough of archers without killing them ourselves over a temporary loss of nerve.

But Sir William would have his way; being in great pain he was in no mood to be trifled with. Victims were selected and lined up in front of the army. There was not enough rope to hang them all at once so they were hanged in groups on the trees where we had held the enemy. I and several others stayed away on the excuse that we were too busy. But there was no way we could avoid these dangling bodies during the short time there. In front of the trees was the carpet of French bodies that had all been searched for loot. It was a grim sight, the only satisfaction was I knew nobody that had been hanged. Sir Martin on second thoughts had kept his men safe.

From Manour on, the French presented no threat to Brittany and we were not strong enough to invade France. For the rest of the year all was quiet.

To Len's delight we camped close to Fourges. As the autumn got chilly we moved into Fourges castle and town. Everyone was thinking of home.

Sir Martin who was in continuous contact with Royston brought me the news that I had a new son, we had already decided to name him Matthew, both were alright so we had a party to celebrate.

In January 1353 Sir Martin and all his men including myself left Brittany for home.

I was very glad to be home for the winter and with very little to do until the spring John my eldest son, now a sturdy lad of seven, was put to work on odd jobs, looking after my horse and learning archery. I taught him also to ride his grandfather's horse as the weather got better.

All that year into 1354 I was retained by Sir Martin.

Being in Royston among friends and comrades gave me time to think of my future interests when my soldiering came to an end. At thirty years of age I thought that at least my campaign days in France were finished. How wrong I was.

Things military began to pick up in 1355. Sir Martin increased his retainers back to the old level, stepped up training and told us a new expedition was being planned.

He later told us a short sharp expedition was being planned in the warmer climate of southern France; there would be much booty and we would be under the command of the Prince of Wales. The insinuation to Len and I was that if we objected to going we would no longer be retained. Kathleen was not in favour but we had no choice, perhaps after this I might be able to establish a different living.

A child was due in December but again I would not be around. Fortunately Kathleen had family and friends with her like last time.

So in October 1355 with one thousand others I went off as a reinforcement to Gascony.

In the coming campaign we would serve in the advance guard commanded by Earl of Warwick. This time, unlike in Brittany, we had an army led by aristocrat leaders.

There was an addition for Warwick, the earls of Salisbury, Oxford and Suffolk, various Gascon lords and a good crop of our middle rank experienced leaders all under the command of Edward the Prince of Wales a veteran of many actions since Crecy. We expected great things.

We spent all winter and spring getting ready and increasing our numbers. There was the usual negotiating as we prepared. By the summer of 1356 we were more than ready.

Meanwhile at Christmas Sir Martin again informed me that Kathleen had delivered a baby girl and all was well. Kathleen and I agreed in advance that this one, if a girl, would be named Joan. I could now put my mind to the task we had in hand. We finally marched out of Bordeaux on the 6th July amongst cheering and waving. Strict discipline was maintained.

We were some six thousand strong.

"That is hardly enough to fight and conquer France," declared Len. "Too many for a raid, not enough for a major show down, I think there is a crafty plot in hand."

We inquired of Sir Martin if he knew what was intended.

"We are only one of three armies on the move," he replied in confidence. "John of Lancaster and the King himself in Flanders are all moving towards the Loire Valley. When we are all joined up the French will be in trouble. We have three objectives: carry fire and sword to the enemy homeland, join up with the King and John of Lancaster, the third is to meet and defeat the French and bring this interminable war to an end."

I thought to myself that some people would not be happy with an end to the war they were doing well out of. I had not done so bad myself.

We marched in the summer heat at an easy pace until on the 28th we reached the French frontier at a place called Vierzon. From here on it would be pillage and arson and a touch of rape for the women who got in the way.

We stayed in this place for a while as Cardinals came and went in our camp from the French pleading for an end to hostilities. While the Cardinals talked we pillaged and burnt. Our Prince was seeking the location of our armies north of the Loire and of the French army and its intentions. They in fact were between us and Paris and having decided they were strong enough to deal with us they began to move in our direction. On the 14th September we moved off westwards toward Tours. Our intention of crossing here was frustrated by strong French forces and destroyed bridges. The main French army was now closing on our rear.

"I think we have been here before and ended up at Crecy," said Len.

"The Loire is a lot wider and more turbulent than the Somme. I think we are going to have a problem," was my reply. "Where the devil is the King or Lancaster?"

"I wouldn't worry too much, the French always make a pig's ear of it," said Sir Martin. "Our leaders know what they are doing."

"I hope you are right."

Then at Montbazan we turned south. It was obvious we had abandoned the idea of making a junction across the Loire. The enemy was trying to get behind us on the road to Bordeaux. We marched south to Châtellerault and halted for two days in the hope that the King or Lancaster would cross the Loire at Angers and come down to join us. The French were still trying to get between us and Bordeaux so we could wait no longer.

Once our wagons, loaded with supplies and loot, had crossed the bridge at Châtellerault our mounted men at arms left us and set off across the country to catch the extended French column in the flank. They struck the rear guard, their main army and their King was already in Poiters.

Being short of water for the horses we had to stop again.

"I think we have blown it this time," said Len.

"Keep your views to yourself. Our commanders know what they are doing and I don't want you undermining morale before we have even seen the enemy. So shut up!" It was Sir Martin who had caught Len's comment.

The two armies were close to each other, it was becoming increasingly difficult to slip away, we would have to stand and fight no matter what the odds.

On the 19th we formed up and faced the enemy ready for a battle.

The Cardinal of Perigord again appeared in our lines to talk peace. The French were gathering like a great black cloud. Any delay now would favour the French who were growing stronger by the hour.

Our Prince dismissed the Cardinal and rode along the ranks of our army giving words of encouragement as he went.

We of the vanguard commanded by Warwick were on the left of the line, behind a hedge that looked down an incline on the road to Poitiers. Nearly a mile away on our left front was high ground over which we could not see. On our immediate left was marshy ground which would be no good for their mounted men. Salisbury and his division was on our right. The Prince of Wales with his division was

73

in the rear. We archers as at Crecy were in wedges pushed forward on the flanks of the two divisions. We were about six thousand strong, the enemy were three times as numerous.

The main body of the enemy advanced towards us on foot. In front came bodies of enemy cavalry charging towards us. No problem we thought.

There was. They were wearing plate armour, stronger than normal and most of our arrows failed to penetrate.

The Earl of Oxford came galloping down from the Prince. He spoke rapidly to Warwick who then ordered us archers to move rapidly to our left into the marshy ground and face inwards at a sharper angle.

"Never mind the knights, shoot at the rear of the horses. Bring them down!"

The enemy was now upon our men-at-arms so we shot like the devil possessed us. Which he did.

The enemy went down in heaps, screaming horses and struggling knights everywhere. Our line might be ragged due to the sudden move to our left but it was still lethal. The enemy cavalry gave up the job to the advancing mass of footmen.

"Next please," said Len.

This enemy force was closer than normally allowed before we could give it our undivided attention and they pushed into our men-at-arms despite all we could do. The hand-to-hand fighting became very intense and the Prince had to despatch the bulk of his reserves to hold the line while we archers pumped death into the enemies' flanks as fast as we could.

After what seemed hours the enemy pulled back, then began to break up.

We were jubilant. We had won again.

A lull descended in the lethal action as our archers replenished their arrows and took long swigs of water which was now brought forward. Individuals and some camp followers were out in front killing and robbing the knights as well as collecting arrows by the armful. Some knights were now mounting up to go in pursuit with the aim of catching some for ransom. Both Len and I had a private agreement with Sir Martin on that subject. We were resting from our exertions and congratulating each other on our performance when a cry rang out taken up by many others.

"God, God!! Look at that!!"

There coming over the skyline of the ridge was a great wall of Frenchmen. Their shields locked together, banners flying, nearly all on foot with the King John amongst them.

We had not beaten the French army at all, only a part of it.

There was a momentary ripple of anxiety bordering on fear in our lines. How could we cope with that lot after the exertions we had already gone through?

Our leaders conferred while we got ourselves back in order.

Neither the marsh nor the hedge would be as good at holding up thousands of footmen as cavalry. Junior leaders had to quell the jitters that ran through the ranks.

Our leaders then made their decision, the rest of the knights were hurriedly mounting up.

"Whatever are we up to this time?" queried Len.

"We are going to hit them first with our cavalry before they get too close!"

"Now there's a novelty. The French won't like that."

Our mounted knights thundered into the wall of French men who were too closely packed together to defend themselves properly. We archers rushed forward to get a better position then released our deadly missiles at them. The enemy was piling up in heaps as our knights and archers fell upon them. The French were very brave and did everything to stop the rot. The cracking point was a sudden attack on their other flank from the last of the Prince's reserves. Their resistance collapsed and they fled as best they could from the field of battle, pursued as far as Poitiers eight miles away.

On the battlefield those of us left behind roved about looking for loot or prisoners of quality to seize for ransom. The rank and file had no chance of holding a knight or lord for ransom, so many were killed out of hand for money and jewels.

However, Len and I had been promised a share of the ransom if we brought a live prisoner to Sir Martin.

I seized on a young knight who had been wounded and dragged him off to Sir Martin who was well pleased. I was told his name was Joseph Mischige. My graceful retirement loomed in sight.

The most important person of the day to be captured was King John himself. Also there were seventeen great lords and over a hundred knights for good measure, we were in great elation as well could be imagined.

Where was my friend Len, I enquired, and was bluntly told some Frenchman had done for him.

I was struck dumb with horror. It could not be! I rushed off to where they pointed. There I found Len dead on the ground, blood all over his body. I was dazed. This could not be true. It was a bad dream.

"That bastard there did him in. Your friend leaned over him to see if he was dead and he had a concealed dagger. We killed him on the spot but that was too late for your friend." The dead Frenchman was a knight.

I was badly shaken.

With the help of others I lifted Len onto my shoulders and carried him back to our place behind the front line.

The joy of victory died then and there for me. Killing nameless strangers at a distance was one thing but this brought home the blood and gore and the stupid futility of war.

The Prince claimed at least three thousand of the enemy died compared with only forty of our own. We did not believe that, so why should others? He was probably only counting the English dead even though half the army was Gascon.

We marched back to Bordeaux where there was much feasting drinking and jollity with girls all around. I was morose and depressed, though I joined in with them disposing of surplus unwanted loot that belonged to Len and I.

In England there were fetes, feasting, ringing of bells and public masses. The French army had been smashed again and their King was a prisoner heading for London.

Throughout the summer and autumn France slid into anarchy while we made merry. Negotiations began again. The French were terrified we would attack them again in 1337 so they signed a treaty in March to last for two years. The ransom for Joseph Mischige was quickly paid. Sir Martin must have asked for too little. However, I got my share and put half of it by with Len's profits.

With no campaign in prospect I returned to England that same month with Sir Martin. I wanted to see the latest daughter I had not seen, it stirred memories of the son I had not seen and, by association, Isobel Jaifrok.

Chapter Six

I was glad to be back in Royston with my family but it was always an embarrassment to meet Len's widow. Like Kathleen she always thought that we would look after each other and come home safe together as before. I gave her more than Len's share of what we had made out of the expedition but it made little difference. He was gone.

The year passed slowly for there was not a lot for us to do. It looked to most people as though the war was over. We had given the French a good thrashing every time we put our minds to it. We held the King prisoner and the country had collapsed into chaos under an ineffective regent. They came to London to talk peace and to get their King back. We talked about the price.

I hoped now that my soldiering days were over but I still kept myself in trim. I practised my archery, competed in teams rode my horse regularly and engaged in manly sports. It was expected of a soldier.

It was sad that Len had fallen on the last day of active campaigning, killed by a wounded knight he hoped to rob and hand over to Sir Martin for a share of the ransom. It seemed ignoble and unnecessary.

In 1358 Sir Martin sickened and died.

Once more I had no employer. Sir Martin had no son and his nephew inherited everything. He was an active knight but had all the armed retainers that he needed. I was offered a job looking after the horses which I rejected. At the age of thirty it might be difficult to get a job as an armed retainer but I was willing to wait a while and see what turned up. I could look for a civilian occupation. Kathleen thought I should have taken the horse job, but that would be to admit I was over the hill, which I wasn't in my opinion.

It was well that I went to the funeral service for Sir Martin. One of those present was Sir Peter Pitt, a gentleman I had noticed at Poitiers. He came across to me after the service.

"Hullo, I understand you are Thomas Simon and you served at both Crecy and Poitiers. Is that right?"

"Yes sir." I realised at this moment that of the whole lance of Sir Harold back in 1345 I was the only one still alive. I had evaded injury in war as well as the plague.

"I'm Sir Peter Pitt from Hertford. I understand that your new master will not be requiring your services. You will be moving on, I take it."

What had it got to do with him? But one must show respect for one's social superiors.

"Sir, he is not my master; my contract was with Sir Martin. I have not had time to think about what I shall be doing."

"Well I'm looking for an experienced soldier to join my armed retainers. A mounted archer like yourself to command and train a troop. You sound like the fellow I am looking for, you have been recommended to me. What do you say? The usual remuneration and accommodation for your family. I understand you have a family."

"Yes sir, a wife and three children."

"Well would you be interested? Hertford is a much more lively place than Royston."

"Well sir, are you training and getting ready for a campaign in Spain or somewhere?" I didn't want any more war. There was also the question of what he meant by 'usual remuneration' for in these post-plague days neither wages nor prices were normal. I did not raise that point yet.

"No, nothing like that but we soldiers should be ready if the King requires us for something."

It did not take much mulling over. It sounded just what I wanted now that Sir Martin was gone. There was nothing around here that really interested me.

"Yes sir, I would be interested."

So the iron dice rolled again.

Kathleen and I with our children moved to Hertford within a week and settled in quickly.

The rest of the year was a doddle. I still had money left from the Poitiers campaign and the ransom of Joseph Mischige. Most soldiers and civilians looked up to me as an experienced veteran, my peers listened to what I had to say. Sir Peter consulted me on matters of training and minor tactics as well as the progress of individuals in my troop. I was welcome at the Manor House. I had acquired status.

Kathleen and the children settled in well, she now did odd jobs at the manor such as sewing and embroidery and seemed to have integrated well, though I sensed at times she was homesick for her family and friends at Royston.

I would often go hunting with Sir Peter which was good exercise and fun. I also kept up to standard with archery and other activities. Sir Peter was quite pleased that I could read and write and though I was very rusty he insisted that I brush up on that.

Though all seemed well I was aware that at thirty-five years of age it was time to think of something different to soldiering.

It would pay me to work on Sir Peter with a view to acceptable employment in his household in the future. In the meantime I got on with being a soldier and training young men that came into my troop. I also trained the young male relatives of Sir Peter in unarmed combat, all of which brought me into contact with a wider range of people.

Hertford being a county town had much more activity and opportunity than Papworth or Royston. Perhaps in time something might turn up to my benefit in the general community. For the moment all seemed well.

The following year, 1359, things changed.

The peace negotiations failed and the Commissioners of Array were out again as they had been fourteen years before.

"If there is to be another campaign in France I shall want you with me," said Sir Peter, which was a compliment of some sort that I did not really want.

"Are you sure I'm not too old for charging about France?" I was slower in my movements and, though he didn't know it, I had a touch of trouble with my knee joints.

"Rubbish! You are one of the fittest and most experienced men I have. No way will I leave you behind. You want to see Paris this time don't you?"

"Yes sir, it would be good to be in at the end."

I could hardly say otherwise and he didn't have to mention the Commissioners of Array.

As the year wore on our forces everywhere grew, training stepped up. Stores, horses and wagons were collected. It seemed to me there was more activity than in the Crecy campaign.

There were delays and cancellations. We were due to leave Hertford in July which was running things late. There were last minute negotiations with the Cardinals, more time was needed to get the things the army needed and to raise the naval force to transport us across the Channel.

At last in late August we began our move. I was not too happy about leaving my family this time and I promised Kathleen it would be the last time. If I came back as rich as I had from the Poitiers campaign I would be set for life and Sir Peter would have to find a replacement for me, but I could hardly back out this time. It was no ordinary expedition.

So off we went, our destination was Dover and from there anywhere that the King might decide. We marched at a steady pace down to London where we were cheered and feted. After two days there we marched down to Canterbury, it was on this stretch of journey that my knees started giving me real trouble and I spent more time in the saddle than most. In the preparations to move, it showed up and Sir Peter noticed all this. We marched on to Dover and into a large tented camp. If we thought we would embark in a few days we were mistaken just like at Portsmouth. This time it was not the weather; the preparations were taking longer.

We were now placed in the Earl of Lancaster's division and informed that we were going to Calais. This brought a strange jump in my interest. Would Isobel Jaifrok and my son Simon still be there? He must be about twelve years old now. Had Isobel told him of me?

The King and his commanders made no secret of our destination.

I enquired of Sir Peter about our options once we got to Calais.

"We are going to put an end to French insolence once and for all. We are going to march straight on to Rheims, the ancient capital of Clovis and there Edward will be crowned King of France, as is his right."

I wondered who Clovis was but instead asked how far it was from Calais to Rheims.

"About one hundred and seventy miles inland. We cannot be supplied from the sea which is why we have had to collect all these heavy wagons and draught horses. We are not likely to get much forage on the way because France is in chaos and destroying its own livelihood."

I had wondered why we had such a vast number of wagons. Now I knew.

"The King doesn't mind who knows. If the French decide to try and stop us, good! We shall give them another Poitiers. If they fail to challenge us or stop us the French people will see that they would be better off as loyal subjects of King Edward. End of war!"

Though I was interested in the plans of my superiors for the final campaign I was growing more interested in Calais and Isobel.

All through September we fretted at Dover. Tournaments, contests and training were organised to keep us occupied.

Across the water, with the King's encouragement, mercenaries and adventurers were drifting into Calais: they expected fine pickings when the campaign started. There were Germans, Flemish and many others. Once there they fretted and got restless and became an annoyance to the locals. They devoured much of the available food and elbowed their way into the best quarters.

At last, on the 1st of October, we sailed.

With our arrival it was decided that something would have to be done about the mercenaries for they were causing much trouble in Calais and hindering us.

Lancaster's plan was to take these people out on a raid into France which would run their surplus energy off and give him time to instil some discipline into them. He also took a large part of his division with him.

Fortunately for me Sir Peter and his command stayed in Calais, for my knee had become quite swollen during our stay at Dover.

Every day troops, wagons and stores were coming across the Channel keeping us all busy. It was by far the biggest expedition we had launched against France yet. Eventually I found time to go in search of Isobel. It was no problem, she was still in her same little house. She was working on her allotment when I arrived. With the movement of boundaries she was in the English enclave.

We were so pleased to see each other that we kissed and embraced joyfully in the allotment. Let the neighbours make of it what they would. She then took me by the hand and chattering happily all the way she led me into her house. I was expecting a young boy to show himself, but nobody was there.

81

Once inside and out of sight we kissed more passionately and the years dropped away. Just the sight of her and the Genii was out of the bottle. I was back.

Not wanting to be interrupted I had to ask.

"Where is Simon? Is he alright?"

After a pause she answered slowly.

"Simon died in the plague back in 1349."

That set a damper on both of us.

But we soon cheered up because life has to go on and we were so pleased to see each other after all these years. Simon was one of many that had died in the Great Plague. It reminded me of my wife and children. The memory of those years was too painful to dwell on.

Although she was in good health, Isobel had had a hard time until recently when the arrival of the expedition and our allies began. She was still selling vegetables, milk, the odd chicken or goose and now and again a kid goat. Although she did all the work herself, she only had herself to feed.

We drank a flagon of wine together and talked of old times until dusk began to fall and it was time for me to return. Much against our will.

As I limped back to my billet I ran into Sir Peter.

"Simon, I think you are pushing things too hard; you are going to knock yourself up before the campaign has begun."

"Oh I shall be alright, just a little stiffness in the knee, sir."

"You take the next couple of days off and rest up. You're not as young as you used to be."

I thought what a good idea. I could rest up with Isobel and nobody would know I was missing.

So next morning I rode out to Isobel with a mounted archer from my troop. I told him to take my horse back and look after it. He was to return the day after tomorrow and in the meantime tell nobody where I was.

I took with me a flagon of wine and a skinned rabbit.

We ate and drank, talked and laughed and when the curfew came down we went to bed and made love regularly. Like me she was more than willing. There were further activities in the night and again in dawn's early light. We would gladly have stayed in bed all day but she had work to do.

She had noticed my knee was not too good, so after breakfast she made me sit in a chair by the door in the sunshine while she got on with her various chores in sight of me. Passing neighbours seemed quite friendly. Soon in the warm sun I dozed off.

"Tommy! Tommy! Wake up!" I heard her say. It was early afternoon. She gave me a cup of wine and came and sat with me. She was concerned about how long I would be in Calais.

"Once the King arrives with the rest of the expedition we shall be off to Rheims."

"Why Rheims? It is far away."

"Our King wants to get himself crowned, then all the fighting will be over. England and France will be one kingdom."

"I don't think you will make it all that way and back on that knee of yours."

"Oh I shall be alright once the marching begins," I said without conviction.

"What would happen if you said you could not march?"

"If they think I'm not up to it they could send me back to England and I would be finished as a soldier. What would I do then?"

"I worry about you," was all she could say.

"What does your forecasts say about me then?"

"I shall look that up this week."

We finished off the last of the rabbit and went to bed early for we had a lot of lost time to make up.

Again we were late up. Then at noon the archer appeared trailing my horse.

"I told you late afternoon, not mid-day!"

"I know sergeant but Sir Peter sent me; he wants to see you right away."

"You should have told him that you didn't know where I was."

"I did but he wouldn't listen. He threatened to flog it out of me."

"Oh very well. I wonder what he wants?"

Isobel and I said a long goodbye and off I went.

At first Sir Peter was irate with me.

"I told you to rest up, not go galloping off after some French wench! You'll be fit for nothing!"

"She is no wench! She is an old friend from the days of the siege. I decided I could rest better there than camp. She looks after me!" I was annoyed that he thought I was wenching, even though in reality I was.

"It's no good you being miles away getting waited on when I want you here! Next time you ask before you go wandering off after your French friend!"

"Yes sir!" At least he was not going to stop me seeing Isobel like Sir Harold had.

It was true there was much to be done. The nearer the time came to take the field the more I worried about my knee seizing up altogether.

Then on the 28th October the King himself arrived with the last division. Lancaster was recalled with his mercenaries. They began to agitate for a fixed wage dated back to when they said they arrived in Calais. The English were not prepared to pay so starting with the Germans they packed up and went home.

The largest army the English had ever sent to France was now coiled like a spring waiting for the word. There were the usual three divisions, one commanded by the Earl of Lancaster, one by the Prince of Wales and the other by the King, a total force of nearly twenty thousand fighting men plus various camp followers. Orders were now issued. Strict discipline was to be maintained, no arson and the death penalty for rape. No wonder the mercenaries had gone home – they must have heard these orders before we did.

Sir Peter sent for me. Expecting more detailed orders, I hurried along to his quarters and found I was alone with him.

"Sergeant, I want you to stay behind here in Calais! There is much to be done in securing stores and directing reinforcements. I need somebody who can read and count and has sufficient authority and experience. That means you!"

"Surely when we march out there will be nothing of ours left behind?"

"I am not just talking of my command but of all the units in the division. You will be billeted in the castle. You have been selected!" That was it. I was dismissed.

Secretly I was very pleased. My knees would not be put to a severe test. I would be snug in the castle while the others would be marching about in the rain and mud, and there would be no loot to cheer them up. I had seen my share of battle and bloodshed though I would like to be in at the end. Another factor to cheer me up was that I would be near to Isobel for several months. I tried to hide my delight. Isobel was more than pleased.

So I watched from the walls of the castle as our army marched out of Calais. There was much singing and cheering for spirits were high. If the French could not beat our much smaller armies in the past then with their country in chaos and virtually leaderless they were not going to stand a chance against this force. Lancaster's division lead the way. Everyone commented on the vast number of heavy wagons that were going.

The day after they all left the autumn rains began. Thereafter the weather became abominable. To start a campaign this late in the year was unheard of but that was the way it happened. The King was not prepared to wait; the French problem had to be sorted out now, the army could not sit about until the spring.

Calais now became the quietest it had been for many months.

I got Isobel to move into a house near the castle. With the main force gone and few senior officers about, things became quite relaxed. I was not the only one blessed with female company.

We lived well, Isobel's land was now fallow and friends looked after the livestock, so we were together in the dry while thousands of others squelched along the road to Rheims.

The news came through in time that our army had reached Rheims but had failed to capture it. A siege began. The French had avoided a major action for they knew what the result would be. A dribble of sick men began to drift back to us as the year wore on with the army in the open.

It was now that I had plenty of time to question Isobel about her prophesies.

"I do not have visions; I ask questions and get answers. I don't know how it is done. I was not able to forestall or foretell the death of our son. I did know that you were going to return to me a week before you arrived. I do know that the war will end next year."

Everyone was forecasting that.

"How will it end?"

"Not by blood but by agreement. After the war you will find employment with somebody who is very important and all will be well with you and your wife."

"You must be careful of who you say these things to or you could be arrested as a witch or something."

"I tell nobody but you."

On another occasion we spoke of the immortality of the soul and reincarnation. I had never heard of this until I met her.

"We shall meet again in a future life, our relationship will probably be different. Death is but a change of form which will change again at rebirth. Our journey is on-going. There will probably be several more lives together before all is resolved."

"What then?"

"We move on to a higher plane."

"If we will meet over several lives in the future, have we not met in the past?"

"Oh yes. I expect so."

I found all this disturbing. I had been brought up to believe in one God, Heaven and Hell. I still went to church every week, but I dared not go to confession.

Isobel went to church as well so as not to draw attention to herself; she did not feel in anyway involved. To her we had to sort ourselves out in a series of lives. We were responsible for our own progress. No priest could absolve us for our sins. We must pay the price in another life.

Surely sooner or later somebody would take notice of what she was saying, although she was very discreet. Then fearful trouble would fall upon her head. I was very concerned about her safety. I wanted to seek out somebody I could talk to but dare not.

After such talks, I would avoid her for a while for she left my mind in a whirl and I was also fearful for my own safety and salvation if I was caught with her in a clash with the Church.

"There is a higher form of existence for the soul but we have to get it right at this level first, and we cannot do that in one lifetime. We also need the experience of different forms of life."

It all sounded very strange to me. Was she a witch, a wizard and agent of the devil sent to catch me?

"We shall not be judged by one God sitting on a throne but by ourselves and our peers."

I suppose I should take comfort from the idea that I would not have to face eternal fire and damnation.

Meanwhile our army laid siege to Rheims until January then gave up and moved south into the warmer friendlier lands of Burgundy for the rest of the winter.

If Edward wanted to be King of France he could hardly storm Rheims and put the inhabitants to the sword then expect to be welcomed by the French. There was not the sustenance in the region for him to stay long, soldiers were already falling sick at an increasing rate. So it was a case of retreat, which would have serious effects, or move south then return in the spring.

So we in Calais were left wondering what would happen next. Not that I was worried, I had Isobel, there was not too much work, a more tolerant easier system than in the field or with a field unit. We celebrated Christmas in style and, like others, I smuggled my lady into the castle for the jollities and feasting and lustful nights while those in charge turned a blind eye because most of them were doing the same.

With the coming of spring, Isobel went off to her house to do the spring sowing and other chores but she always came back for the weekends, and quite often we spent them tucked up in the castle.

There was an increase in rumours as the weather improved; we were all waiting to see how the war would develop in the campaign season. Before long we heard that our army in Burgandy was on the move towards Paris and hopes rose for a grand climax. But our army did not attack Paris and the French did not attack our army. The King marched around the place. Then negotiations opened at Bretigny. These negotiations were not about a truce or armistice but about peace! Isobel was right again.

In May of 1360 the two sides met to talk, for it had become too costly to keep going. I was not the only one who had to give serious thought to what I would do if my services were no longer required.

The army returned to Calais and I left the castle to return to Sir Peter's command. I was not too happy about my prospects: Sir Peter had already decided last year that I was no longer fit for service in the field, all the talk about maintaining the base was a sop to get me out of the front line. Now the war was over he would have his pick of fit young men.

After much worry, with Isobel telling me all was going to turn out right I decided to take the bull by the horns and approach Sir Peter.

"Sergeant," he said. "I have given some thought about what is to happen not only to you but others in my service. Obviously I cannot keep everybody who wants to stay in my service. I have over the last weeks spoken to various people in authority and I can tell you that your situation and opportunities are different. You are a veteran with experience in command, you have organising ability and are literate. We still need people like you. If you are interested I can recommend you for a post that has come up in the King's service. You are getting too old for field service but there is a place for you at Dover castle that you might like."

"Dover castle? Whatever would I do there?"

"You will be a Gaoler in the King's service. It's a permanent post that will last you for years regardless of wars or the lack of them. You deserve it after years of faithful service. You are immensely suitable but you will have to get in quick before others get in. What do you say to that?"

There was no doubt in my mind that service in such a prestigious place as Dover Castle would be ideal and a bit of a sinecure.

"Yes sir," I said after a suitable pause. "I would like you to put me forward for that post. Thank you very much for telling me about it."

So wheels were set in motion.

Isobel and I knew we could not stay together when the war was over but I would only be over the Channel twenty miles away, there would surely be opportunities to see each other even though my wife and family would be in Dover.

I stayed in Sir Peter's command all through the summer as our army melted away. Then in September came the reply. I was accepted into Royal service at Dover as a Gaoler on seven pence a day all found. Great!

I wrote to Kathleen and told her what was happening and to be ready to join me shortly. She could not read and write herself but the bailiff always helped out in such things.

Isobel in parting warned me not to mention her to Kathleen. We should with luck meet again without upsetting anyone.

"In any case we will meet again in a future life, of that I am sure." These were her parting words after out last night together. I wondered if she was pregnant but didn't ask.

At last I went with Sir Peter and his retinue over to Dover where we stayed a night together to celebrate my entry into the King's service, our return to England and the end of a long war.

Next morning Sir Peter paid all my arrears of pay and took his horse back off me. We did not come back with much plunder compared with other expeditions, in fact having spent all my time in

Calais I came back with nothing. But I did have better prospects than ever before.

I watched my comrades ride away then I went to present myself to the guard commander at Dover castle.

Chapter Seven

So a new chapter in my life began. Once inside the castle and my credentials checked I was taken to the Chief Gaoler. He was a tough-looking man, taller and broader than I. He welcomed me, shook my hand and invited me to sit down. The room was rather dingy, a torch flickered on the wall and a dull autumn light came in through a narrow slit. There were several other people in the room, sitting quietly watching and listening.

"So you are Thomas Simon are you? Served at Crecy and Poitiers, fifteen years military service. A mounted archer no less. Well I'm Mister Mitchell, your immediate superior. I am in charge of the prison complex and all and everything in it. You will always address me as Mister Mitchell. For the first year here you are on probation. One word from me and you are out. Understand?"

"Yes Mister Mitchell."

"All of us here have long military service and are literate." He paused and looked intently at me.

"I served at Crecy also." Another pause.

"All told there are ten of us here and eleven prisoners. Some of the prisoners are actually knights and the rest are gentlemen of means. We have no riff raff in here, this is a royal castle not a heap of stones."

I had never heard of knights being held prisoners by their own people. How odd. He went on to explain the system which operated to keep an eye on them.

"You work in threes for twenty-four hours at a time. Visitors and food are allowed in under supervision. When not on duty you can, in reason, go anywhere in the castle but you will not leave without my permission. Any questions?"

"Not at the moment Mister Mitchell but I expect some will come to me as I move around."

He then introduced me to my two companions who would serve with me and one or two others that were in the room.

"Your room mates will tell you what you need to know, show you around and get you sorted out. Your first duty is tomorrow at sunrise."

We stood up, drained our flagons and he handed me over to the others. They showed me where my room was and the stores, refectory and tailors, and saw that I was fitted out as a royal gaoler complete with a new dagger and knuckledusters.

"Do you get out of this place often?" I asked.

"We get out every three days. Mister Mitchell is the only one who is allowed to have his family in the castle. The rest of us have our families outside in a hostel for castle families only, all together in case of trouble."

"Trouble? What trouble?"

"I have been here for five years and we have had no trouble to cause families to be moved, so don't worry about it."

The following day, having been woken by a fellow gaoler, I began my duties.

The first task was checking and counting the prisoners. The doors to their cells were opened so that they could move about in the complex and socialise with each other as long as they did not attempt to go further. Breakfast of sorts was given them, same as we got.

Most were arrogant snobs that tried to talk down to us jailors, especially a new one like me.

"Don't let them rattle you. You have the keys not them, and we can make life difficult if they go too far and they know it," said my companion.

One of us would sit on a stone seat for two hours at a time facing down to the cells, the other two were in an alcove nearby within easy speaking distance.

I thought it might be boring but I soon learnt to watch and assess as well as keep track of who was where. Their snobby manners were an education. It was like watching fish. Being of independent means the prisoners sent out for food, wine and other things; they didn't want to eat like us. Sometimes they flaunted their goods before us. There was always at least one with a visitor, not counting servants. With all this coming and going I was surprised that some didn't try to get away.

Several times a day Mister Mitchell would come round to see that all was in order. At the changing of the castle guard in the morning the guard commander and the duty officer of the day would come and look at the prisoners and us. It gave the impression that the soldiers looked upon prisoners and gaolers as all the same people. However I was proud to be in the King's service.

So time rolled on. Kathleen and the children came and lodged in the hostel near the gate with the others. John being fifteen years of age had taken service in Huntingdonshire. The family would now begin to shrink like families do.

We made lots of new friends. Kathleen was happy with the situation and did odd jobs for the castle and the hostel.

Christmas was a jolly affair and the winter caused no problems.

The war was supposed to be over but there was still fighting here and there, off and on. Pirates roamed the Channel from French ports. In England there was much unease aggravated by unemployed soldiers, sailors and others. Disturbances over wages and prices caused by the dislocations of the plague still rumbled on. A new generation was growing up that was not so amenable to authority.

Mister Mitchell was very adamant about our position. We were the King's men and were in no way to get involved in social and political controversies. We would carry out the orders passed down to us. The reason for well-shod people being prisoners was no concern of ours.

"Do what you are told and keep your mouth shut or you are out. Lots of people want your job so keep your nose clean!"

Being old soldiers, one and all, we had no problem with that. We had a regular living wage, our families comfortably housed nearby, we were all fed and well clothed. What more could a working man want?

I got on well with Mister Mitchell and my fellow gaolers, especially my room mates. The great kitchen fascinated me especially with its lifts to take food while still hot up to the various apartments as quickly as possible. The water system was a wonder to behold. Water from a very deep well was pumped into every part of the castle. The store rooms were by far the largest I had ever seen. If an enemy wanted to starve us out he would have a long job. The massive castle was a labyrinth of passages, stairs, rooms and battlements where a newcomer could easily get lost. I was happy wandering around in my spare time, seeking and talking. I had never seen such a wonderful place. The view across the Channel was superb.

Mister Mitchell was right, most castles were just heaps of stone in comparison. Even Calais could not match it.

Outside the gates were my wife and children. All was well with the world. Though the stone steps didn't do my knees much good nobody seemed to notice.

Some eighteen months after I had become gaoler Mister Mitchell sent for me.

"I have a little job for you. You are to go to Calais to pick up a prisoner and bring him here. You will have three soldiers with you as escort but you alone will be responsible for the prisoner. You will leave tonight and return tomorrow, weather permitting. Understood?"

"Yes Mister Mitchell."

He then told me the name of the prisoner, which meant nothing to me, handed over a pass to Calais and authority to collect the prisoner.

"What has he done?"

"That is none of your business. Just bring him back here in one piece!"

So that night I and three others crossed the Channel to Calais and reported to the castle. On the way I briefed the escort on what I expected of them, but my mind was turning to Isobel Jaifrok.

In the morning the sea had turned rough so we were not able to return. Not having yet taken responsibility for the prisoner I left the castle telling everyone I was just going round the corner to see an old friend. That incited some nudging and winking, but I paid no heed. Isobel was increasingly on my mind since this task was mentioned. To my surprise she was at her gate expecting me. Clinging to her skirt was a toddler. We were both full of joy and embraced warmly.

"How did you know I was coming?"

She did not answer. I picked up my son, also named Simon, and hugged him close. We went indoors and talked happily. Simon was nervous at first but soon came round.

I told here about my job as gaoler and why I was here.

"I knew you would come again. I'm so glad you are not a soldier anymore. I would like to see you now and again."

I returned to Calais Castle in the late afternoon. The weather did not improve so we were still delayed. That night I stayed with Isobel. It was like old times.

As we lay together warm and naked in dawn's early light, Isobel brought our light conversation round to the subject of the eternal soul.

93

"Be not afraid of death, it is only a change of form. We shall not be parted for long."

"Why do you talk of death? We have little time together, let us be cheerful."

"We shall have many centuries together. What is more cheerful than that."

"Well I have no intention of dying yet. I'm under forty years of age. If you say there is no death then that's alright by me."

She tried to tell me of some prophesy but I did not want to hear, time was too short, and though she was turned forty she had a lovely soft, warm body, so I rolled her on her back and let passion have its way.

The weather was clearing and it was obvious that some time today I would return across the Channel. We parted with a heavy heart.

I collected the prisoner and was back in Dover by nightfall. The sea was still choppy but we got across alright though most people were seasick.

The prisoner was a gentleman of refinement; he tried several times to strike up a conversation but I ignored him. I neither knew nor cared what he was supposed to have done, for Isobel was whirling around in my mind together with Kathleen and my children.

Prisoners came and went but some seemed to stay for ever. We could watch with amusement the petty intrigues, bickering, and changing friendships. Being good gaolers we sometimes set off clashes between them for divide and rule was our objective. If they all saw eye to eye they would combine against us and they were not dumb peasants and each had family and friends outside. Sometimes it reached the point where we did have to step in and separate contending parties, for life in their condition was a social hot house. If they did harm each other, we would have trouble.

One thing I missed most at Dover was riding through the countryside. I had no horse for the first time in years. I could on occasion practise my archery but it was not like the intense competitions I had been used to. However, life must go on through changing phases. At least I was in reasonably good health for my age.

Some three years later, just after Matthew had left home to be a seaman, Mister Mitchell sent for me again to go and fetch another prisoner from Calais.

My heart leapt at the thought of seeing Isobel and my son again. I know not why for the relationship with my wife Kathleen was very good. Why did I, a happily married man, want a foreign woman who was showing signs of age and likely to end up at the stake?

Nevertheless I stayed another night in Calais and spent it with Isobel and my son. We were late to bed because Simon would not go to sleep; he was upset at someone else being in his mother's bed. Then our passion was unleashed and I knew I could not give her up.

Simon woke us early and I had to be off. There was the same depression at leaving. This could not go on. It could not amount to anything. I had a good wife and family and my place was in Dover. This so weighed me down and interfered with my concentration that I went to church and confessed my sins to a priest. Though he sounded sympathetic and understanding, he still gave me punishment to cleanse my soul. Then he warned me not to go to Calais again but to find some excuse next time. He also suggested that if Kathleen was pregnant it would take my mind off Isobel. I thought that might be risky with Kathleen now thirty-five years old, and what did I want with a screaming infant. He also said that if the authorities found out about my long-term liaison with a foreign woman I might be posted to some other royal castle or even dismissed from the service. The idea of being posted away possibly to Carlisle did not appeal though I did not believe I would be dismissed, too many of my seniors were doing the same thing.

I tried to banish Isobel from my mind but she kept on coming back. I loved her and she had the allure of forbidden fruit.

In 1369 the war with France broke out again. Security was tightened up but there was no major battle.

One day in 1372 we heard we were to have a new Constable, not the first change since I had arrived, for the post was a plum of political intrigue, but it did prove to be important to me. In due time Lord Latimer arrived.

On his arrival he insisted on inspecting every part of the castle and everyone in it and its capabilities as though he expected some sort of crisis in the offing. His minions were poking everywhere.

Then two weeks later Mister Mitchell and I were sent for by one of the Constables' senior officers. I had never been in that part of the castle before. It was quite a sumptuous apartment we were led to, unlike our bleak, stone rooms. This room, although stone, was covered in carpets and tapestry; there was more light and air from the wider windows.

The officer we were lead to came bluntly straight to the point.

"Thomas Simon you will take the place of Mister Mitchell forthwith. You will have the salary, authority and responsibilities that he has had, you will have the quarters for your family that he has and whatever benefits go with the post of Chief Gaoler. Mister Mitchell is dismissed the King's service. Any questions?"

It was blunt to the point of brutal. I was quite taken aback, I had not been prepared for this.

I stammered something that he paid no attention to.

"You will give a written report on your command by tomorrow morning!"

The over-dressed, nasty looking character then dismissed us with a wave of the hand. These new people were not the type of gentlemen I served with in the army.

On our way back to the prison complex I asked Mister Mitchell if he knew the reason for this abrupt dismissal – what was he guilty of?

"It is all about settling old scores, Mister Simon. I knew I was in trouble soon as I saw who was on Lord Latimer's staff. Nothing for you to worry about. I don't know what Mrs Mitchell will say."

It was the first time I had been addressed as Mister Simon, it sounded quite odd after spending twelve years as a nobody.

Kathleen was very pleased at our elevation and soon moved into the castle with Joan. Norman had already gone off to seek his fortune like a young man should.

Now after twelve years in the King's service I was in charge of the prison complex, the other gaolers, and prisoners who now numbered seven. My wages increased together with the perks and authority. I had much better quarters and could see my wife every day. I was now dressed better and permitted to wear a short sword as a symbol of my new rank when in the castle. If a prisoner or gaoler got out of hand I still had my dagger and knuckledusters to bring them back into line. But because they knew I would use them if need be I had no trouble. If anything, the gaolers were more frightened of me than the prisoners.

Things were better for me and Kathleen but Joan was not too happy: at seventeen she felt isolated from her old friends.

"I think we ought to let her stay with friends in the town occasionally, she will come to no harm and it is time she found a young man," said Kathleen.

I was not in favour; she was my only daughter and the last child still at home. Surely there were suitable young men in the castle service; the place was in fact full of them.

"That is not the same thing. She doesn't want us watching her all the time. She doesn't have to leave home, just stay with friends now and again. Nothing permanent."

I was not happy with the idea but they had obviously been having a chat. They were right. If you want to keep your children then you must let them go. And so it was Kathleen and I were left together alone more often.

As Chief Gaoler there was no reason why I should not go and collect prisoners from Calais but I never did. I always sent a competent gaoler instead. I knew if I went I would be in Isobel's arms in short order. It would be painful to us both. Now I was with Kathleen every night I was content for I was not an adulterer by nature.

Then one day, about a year after my promotion, a messenger was brought to me. He worked for one of the local traders that supplied our prison. He said there was a woman in a tavern outside who urgently wanted to see me – would I come at sundown? Now who could that be? The messenger did not know. He had not seen her; he had been given a groat to come and tell me.

Was it somebody from Kathleen's family with bad news? Could it be Isobel? There was only one way to find out.

I went to the tavern in question just after sundown.

It was Isobel.

All sorts of things raced through my mind. Did she intend to move over here and install herself outside the castle? Had she come to expose me to Kathleen? Had she come to get money off me?

"Hello Tom. I hope you don't mind me coming. I know you will not be coming to Calais again." The voice was as seductive as ever.

We kissed discreetly in a small alcove. Then I got myself a flagon of ale and a red wine for her and sat down with her. We held hands under the table and talked quietly.

"Isobel, I can hardly come to you at night. I live with my wife in the castle, and I'm too well known around here."

"No, no! I don't want to come between you and your wife or cause you embarrassment. In any case I am fifty-two years old now. No, I just want to see you and talk to you again because I love you."

So we stayed and talked, she promised to bring my son next time. We warmed to each other as we sat there and we agreed we should set up some kind of communication so that we did not completely lose each other. I had to leave her before curfew, so once more we parted and there were tears in her eyes.

For several days I could not look Kathleen in the eye. Did she suspect something? But as I never went out alone for some time after that, any suspicions she had must have died away.

The 1370s became more turbulent as they advanced. An English army was soundly beaten in Spain. Raiders were more active in the Channel and in 1377 our beloved King died. Prince Edward was already dead so the crown passed to the late King's grandson, a mere boy named Richard.

In the same year I had a message from Simon that Isobel had died. I did not need him to tell me for I felt the very moment she went. Simon was now sixteen years old so I sent him a sum of money to help him out. It was the least I could do.

In the late 70s the powers that be decided to bring in a Poll Tax on every one over fourteen years of age. The turbulence accelerated alarmingly and there was difficulty in raising it. The government decided to press on. They needed the money they said and the rich people and merchants were objecting to any increase in their share, the pressure on the people was increased.

Then in 1381 the unbelievable happened. All across the land the peasants rose in revolt. The authorities were caught off their guard. We in Dover Castle had insufficient strength to march out and confront the rebels in Kent, there was in any case French raiders ready to pounce. Rochester Castle fell to the rebels and we had to look to our own security. Great hordes of rebels, many of them ex-soldiers and sailors, converged on London from Kent and Essex.

The world had turned upside down.

Then all of a sudden it was over, law and order was restored, authority re-established and ring leaders hunted down ruthlessly. But never again would a government take such liberties with the people for a long time. Their arrogance had been shaken.

It was some time after that that I began to develop some sort of lung trouble which, with my knees, made climbing stairs difficult. I was now at the grand old age of fifty-seven so what could one expect?

I was often confined to bed in the damp weather. Kathleen was worried to death about me and my daughter Joan, now married, often dropped in to see me when I was not well. To my surprise they kept me on until I was sixty-two. By then my assistant was doing most of my duties.

We had had a good run, my wife and I, and we rented a small cottage on the edge of town.

With me unable to work any longer and only a small pension, Kathleen applied for parish relief. She was told we were not their responsibility, if we wanted relief we must go to my place of birth, Papworth. Then they added 'You are better off than most, be thankful'. This upset Kathleen but it was true. What worried me was how Kathleen would manage when I died. In Papworth she could get help as my widow. So we returned to Papworth, mainly on traders wagons, to live with my widowed sister Helen. I was back where I started.

The journey from Dover was too much for me, then the winter did further damage with the result that I died on the 10th of March 1387 on our thirty-sixth wedding anniversary. I expired in the arms of my dear wife. It was a tremendous relief.

Isobel Jaifrok, my first wife Isobel, and my old friend Leonard Roper and the others were there to greet me as I arrived on this new plane. All pain and discomfort was gone.

Soon after this my son John joined us. Then eight years later Kathleen arrived. It was time to think of where we had gone wrong and what we could do about it when we reincarnated into humans again.

Nobody in my circle was going to a higher plane of existence.

I decided that I might avoid some of the troublesome temptations of being a male and killing people if I was reborn as a female.

And so it was.

PART 2

Chapter Eight

I was reborn as Mary Jones on 13th June 1407 at Jacobstowe in Cornwall. My father's name was Harold, he was mainly a farm labourer but at this time he was a Fuller. He was born in 1386 and married my mother Grace Davies in March 1406.

There was much turmoil at my birth which resulted in my mother's death. As a result I was taken away to Indian Queens, also in Cornwall, by my paternal aunt Edith Mills.

Edith already had three sons. Alan aged five, John aged three and Peter aged two. Edith, who was thirty-one years old, must have been a motherly sort to take me in when she had three of her own. There were other relatives in the Jacobstowe area, perhaps because I was a girl, perhaps she thought she was better placed and therefore it was her family duty. Perhaps it was my father's persuasion and she was his favourite and the first choice. Or was she the one ordained to bring me into an ongoing circle of people?

Anyway, off I went with Edith who from then on I looked upon as my mother. We got on very well from the start. Her husband John was a year older than she was and an independent small farmer with his own land on which he kept sheep, pigs, poultry and a cow for milk. There was also a vegetable patch so, all told, the family was better off than average.

I was not very popular with Peter, the youngest, because until I arrived he had been the favourite with Edith and he felt his nose had been effectively put out of joint permanently by a baby girl that was the centre of attention. John was a sickly child and rather quiet. Alan took to me straight away like an old friend. He was very pleased to have a little sister. John, my new father, was a jovial type and looked on me as someone special, the only daughter he had, the apple of his eye.

Mother always took me around with her chatting away cheerfully. She told me everything she thought I ought to know, even when I could not understand, but bit by bit I learned.

103

When I was six John died. Mother was most upset though she had suspected the worst for some time.

As well as telling me about household management, cooking, and food preparation she taught me sewing and knitting, all things she said I would need to know when I grew up. I found it all very interesting and would do anything for my parents, especially mother. She told me religious stories, taught me prayers and as soon as I could walk she took me to church every Sunday. She thought I was much more placid than her exuberant boys.

Peter was always trying to look up my skirt; sometimes I would oblige then he got very friendly and generous. It was our little secret.

As soon as the boys were considered old enough they went to help father around the farm. John lasted a week then he died.

At meal times we were all together. After work in the long dark evenings there was not a lot we could do for there was only the light from the fire to see by unless father, as he sometimes did, lit a torch and fixed it to the wall. Going out to the privy in the dark always terrified me. When the longer, warmer days came there always seemed to be more work to do around the farm and house. In the summer months our parents always made spare time for us children to play or do our own thing. I didn't know how lucky we were for those times.

When I was five I no longer slept in my parents' room but was moved to a narrow cubicle, much against my will.

Occasionally our routine would be broken by the arrival of a travelling fair. There was also a market every week to which father would go to sell eggs and vegetables and bring back what he thought we needed.

As I grew older mother would take me up the market to buy something specific which she said couldn't be left to a man. It was also a good chance to gossip with friends and relatives and hear local scandal. The men were more interested to hear of events further afield. Indian Queens stood at the junction of the roads from London and Bristol; eight miles to the north was the coast of Newquay, to the south was St Austell on the other coast. Thus we were not only a crossroad but a bottleneck.

Many were the rumours of pirates, smugglers and shipwreck to keep tongues wagging. Indian Queens was a good sounding board.

The Turner family lived in the Manor House near the church, they owned much of the land around here. They were not only landowners but also the head of the family was a knight. When Sir George rode out it always caused a stir especially if he was in his armour for whatever reason.

When I was six years old I remember we had a new King, said to be very handsome, brave and well-built who went by the name of Henry the Fifth. About this time we also heard of religious controversy in the land. How people could dispute the word of the Lords I knew not, and there were no Lollards in our area to tell us even if we had been prepared to listen. Apparently they were led by a man called Oldcastle who came to a sticky end just as our priest predicted. The men gossiped about such things but to women they were just noising off, nothing to do with them.

Before long, Henry was off to wage war on the French and our Sir George and several others from hereabouts went with him. They soon returned claiming a spectacular victory at a place called Agincourt. There were several celebrations as a result and the men were much excited.

About this time I would accompany my mother to the Manor when extra domestic staff was needed. It was a fascinating stone building. I used to work in the kitchen, mainly washing up. They seemed to eat a tremendous amount of food in the Turner family. There was often juicy titbits left over to sample.

Many local people were beholden to the Turner family but as father often said he was a free yeoman and owed neither goods or services to anyone except for the church tithes.

Life rolled on quite happily in my childhood, as an average yeoman family we were well-fed, well-housed and suitably dressed. We worked long hours at whatever we were put to, but on the odd days we had to ourselves we children found enough energy to enjoy things. At such times Alan was always there as my guardian in the rough and tumble of growing up. Then I reached my teens and things changed.

To my consternation I changed into what mother called a healthy young woman. She tried to explain it all to me but it sounded confusing, frightening and embarrassing because she did not know how to explain properly and had not forewarned me. Then she delivered another bombshell.

"My dear Mary, I think I ought to tell you now before somebody else does. You are not our real daughter."

Trying to cope with the stress of a first menstruation and its implications was bad enough but this was unbelievable.

"Mother, what are you saying? Of course I am your daughter!"

Was she losing her grip on reality?

"No my dear. Your real mother, who was my sister-in-law died when you were born and we took you in as ours."

This was too much for one day and I fled the room. It was the end of my childhood. It left me shaken and afraid of the future. Alan came and found me crying in the chicken coop. Here was somebody I could lean on.

With my head on his shoulder and his arm around me I told him what mother had said about my birth. I could not tell him the awful thing that was happening to my body. He was most comforting; he vaguely remembered my arrival in the family, so mother was not making it up.

"We always have and always will love you. You will always be a part of this family." With Alan I went back to mother who consoled me; she had been shaken by my reaction but now we got over it together though nothing was the same again. Peter was now told: he did not remember my arrival, he was still practically a baby himself at the time. He made disapproving noises. They were forbidden to say anything to anybody. Once I had absorbed the fact that I was adopted I wanted to know about my real father. Mother had not seen him since I was about two.

"I think he still lives in Jacobstowe."

"Where is that?"

"Miles away. You will never get there."

Things were changing in the outside world as well. The King died and we had an infant on the throne, Henry the Sixth. There were soon rumours of disputes at the top of the social tree about who should be his guardian, which later grew into slander and threats. This did not concern us but it was fertile ground for gossip.

It was one day when I was in the chicken coop feeling depressed that things took another turn.

Alan came along and tried to cheer me up. I laid my head on his shoulder and had a little weep.

"Let me kiss your tears away."

He kissed my eyes, my forehead, then kissed my lips. Now that was different. I could not but respond. It was very pleasant. Alan was my knight in shining armour. We were not brother and sister. We separated in some embarrassment but held hands for a while and snuggled up close. When we did part, I could not help giving him a quick kiss on the lips.

I was in turmoil for the rest of the week and could hardly sleep at night. I was much confused. Could this be wrong? He was not my brother.

Having started this thing, it was repeated at least once a week in the chicken coop, the kissing became more exciting each time.

Then one week he ran his hand over my growing breasts and I felt a thrill like never before. His hand soon found its way into my bodice which was much more thrilling and the kissing got more passionate. Where would this stop?

I began to worry about our relationship. Somebody was bound to catch us one day; if not, it was only a matter of time before his hands would wander to other parts of my body. I felt very guilty about looking forward to that. I was flowering into a presentable young female and he was irresistible.

The one who caught us out was mother. We did not know and she did not say but shortly she took me to one side.

"My dear girl, I think it is time you had a proper job. You will learn more, be independent, meet more people, probably Mister Right. You cannot do that if you stay at home."

"I don't want to leave home." I was struck with the fear of the unknown.

"I'm not talking of you going miles away. I have had a talk with Mrs Hemmings the cook at the Manor; she is willing to take you on as kitchen maid. The job has prospects and you already know Mrs Hemmings and most of the people in that kitchen so you will be alright."

"I won't have to live at the Manor will I?"

"Yes, my dear you will. But that is no problem; it is only at the end of the town not the end of the world." There was a pause as it all sank in.

"Now get your coat on and we will go and see Mister Hemmings the butler, he will put you right and no doubt have some questions."

It all happened so quickly that I knew not how to stop the process. They all said it would not be much different workwise than at home. I appealed to father but he cheerfully backed mother.

"Give it a whirl," he said. "If you don't like it you can come home. It's only up the road, not in Arabia."

My opinion on the matter did not count. I did not know it was mother's plan to separate me from her son before serious mischief was done. She had told nobody what she had seen in the chicken coop.

Within a couple of days with a small bag, a little money and a tear in my eye I was off to the Manor.

I had a room in the attic with two other servant girls, the previous kitchen maid had in fact gone on to something better. I thought that was not too difficult, I felt abandoned and alone in the world.

They all said it would not be much different to what I was used to and I would be independent.

Mother had been happy, chatty and friendly. She always let me rest when I was tired.

We would sit and talk and plan the day.

In the Manor the working hours were longer and more intense with no time for rest. Mrs Hemmings had no intention of talking to me about the plans for the day, she only gave orders. I'm sure she was a very good lady but she believed the devil would find work for idle hands so she made sure from the day I arrived that my hands were never idle from rising in the morning until bed at night.

Every so often my mother came along on some excuse to see how I was getting on. I was sorely tempted to ask to go home with her, but pride always stopped me. I did not wish to be labelled a quitter. I was expected to knuckle down and earn my keep so I did. After all I was an orphan.

I was told by my mother that Alan was now courting a Joan Piball, a young woman in the town. That made me feel even more abandoned. I cried that night.

I saw very little of the Turner family and was never allowed in their part of the house. Lady Turner would come into the kitchen occasionally to check that all was well or to have a word with the cook but she took no notice of me.

There was extra work at Christmas looking after the Turner family and their guests, then the following day there was half a day of fun for the staff. It was the only time that master and mistress saw all their staff together in the year. It left me more home sick than ever. There were always guests popping in for whom we were required to produce extra food at short notice. Sir George was quite a sociable type and it was us servants who got the extra work.

Starting in the spring I would go with Mrs Hemmings to the market. On these excursions I was expected to remain at her side at all times unless one of my family turned up, when she would leave us for a while to chat about family affairs.

One day Alan turned up. Mrs Hemmings had no objection to us being together out of her sight for a short while. Mother had not told her about Alan and I in the chicken coop.

Alan thereupon wanted to give me a kiss but I turned away.

"I hear you are going strong with Joan Piball," I said coldly.

"Well yes Joan and I do get on well together, and now I'm coming on twenty everyone tells me it's time to settle down but that doesn't mean that I don't love you as well Mary. I miss you. We must not get too involved, we are cousins after all."

"Well I miss you but I don't have anybody interested in me now. I cannot see what being cousins has got to do with anything."

"Well it has, but I shall always be interested in you Mary."

"Is that what you say to Joan and the others?"

"Others! There are no others." That stung him; he was most indignant and I softened towards him. It was not his fault that I was expelled from home. He had until then always been there for me. A young man needs female company everyone said, then what about young women, or was I different to other young women. Being cousins would have caused problems it was true.

At last we held hands and I laid my head on his shoulder.

"I feel so alone and unhappy. What is to become of me?"

"I shall always be here for you and one day you will meet a nice young man."

Then we kissed. It was not like old times but it brightened me up before I went back to Mrs Hemmings.

Perhaps we could meet again more often we agreed.

"I love you," he whispered as I slipped away.

That evening I was more depressed; he was with Joan Piball saying and doing God knows what, while I was in a cold attic. I cried myself to sleep.

As time went on, I became quicker and more knowledgeable in my work which pleased Mrs Hemmings so that she became more friendly and less inclined to nag me. In fact she became quite friendly and chatty. Her husband increasingly looked upon me as his daughter. It was not like being at home waiting for the hungry menfolk to return, but I was learning to accept things as they were.

Mrs Hemmings would now sometimes send me off on my own to market. On such trips I sometimes met mother and stopped for a chat. But it was not like the old times.

Why was it necessary for me to go out into the world to earn a living while two sons older than I still lived at home. I felt I had been rejected for no good reason. I sometimes met father, he was always cheerful, always assuming that things were going well and I was happy. Who was I to confuse him?

Then because they thought it would make me happy, the Hemmings gave me half a day off to attend Alan's wedding to Joan Piball. It was the first time all the family gathered together since I had moved to the Manor. It made me realize more than ever how I had been sidetracked and isolated. Mother tried to be friendly and talked vaguely of my return if I wished in the near future. But I was resentful. Watching the wedding was not pleasing for me either; the groom might be my cousin but I wanted him more than ever. I returned to the Manor lonelier than ever and after the inquisitive chatter of my room mates had ended I cried myself to sleep.

There were other handsome young men in Indian Queens but most were with friends, other females, or riding by on horseback; none gave me a second glance. There were young working men there and at the Manor who would be willing to talk to me but I wanted none of them: I would wait for Prince Charming if I could not have Alan.

Now that I was older and nicely developed, Mrs Hemmings would often say 'Mister Right will come along one day and whisk you away, don't you fret'.

How could Mister Right find me if I was always in the Manor except for odd trips to market?

I had no wish to be a spinster all my life. There must be somebody out there who would whisk me away and make me happy ever after.

Chapter Nine

Then, when I was twenty years old in the year of 1427, things changed.

Sir George was killed in a tournament in Devon. His broken body was brought back and we all attended the funeral.

His son Samuel, who lived elsewhere, returned to claim his inheritance and title.

After the funeral he had all the servants from every part of the Manor gathered together on the lawn at the back of the house so that he could look us over and we could see who was the new boss. He came round to speak to us all in a friendly way moving about with ease and confidence. Beer and cakes were provided to loosen people up. He came to me with a glass in hand and a friendly smile; he was not much older than I.

"Hullo, what's your name and what do you do?"

I curtsied as best I knew and before I could answer Mrs Hemmings spoke up.

"This is Mary Mills, she works with me in the kitchen as a maid."

"A very good looking kitchen maid, if I may say so."

"Thank you, kind sir."

"Are you happy here? Do they treat you properly?"

"Oh yes sir."

How could I say otherwise.

With a smile and a nod of his head he moved on.

As he moved on, my eye caught a handsome young man some distance behind him. I had never seen him before, he must have arrived with Sir Samuel. He was rather tall, well-dressed, but not quite a gentleman. Who was he?

I became aware that he had noticed me also. His eyes looked me up and down approvingly which made my heart flutter. Our eyes met and I lowered my head with a blush like a good maiden should. Perhaps he was the type that took advantage of all young women. Both mother and Mrs Hemmings had warned me of such men.

Who was he? What was his position in the household?

He seemed a cheerful, chatty type and his eyes kept wandering my way. He sensed I might be interested and began to move discreetly in my direction. With Mrs Hemmings standing guard he was not likely to get far.

Before he could get within speaking distance Sir Samuel called him to him. His name was Peter. Sir Samuel introduced him to some of the senior members of the household.

Before Peter could begin his approach to me again, Sir Samuel decided he had been with us riffraff long enough and we were dismissed. Mrs Hemmings quickly shepherded her kitchen staff away; there was much to be done.

Later in the day I queried Mrs Hemmings about who the young man was.

"That is Peter Jenkins, Sir Samuel's valet. You will see more of him at the senior staff dining table when you wait on him. Don't get any ideas, he is not for you."

So it was, the six senior members of staff which included Mr Hemmings, and Mrs Jones the housekeeper were all together around the table and I made it my duty to wait on Peter and to attend to his every wish. Unlike the others he noticed me; his smile and kind words gave me a glow. There was a man I could fancy.

What if he was one of those men I had been warned about. At least he spoke to me. He was a most presentable young man perhaps a little older than I.

After the first few days he took to coming down to the kitchen when he had no real need so that we could have a quick chat. The more I saw of him the more my heart fluttered.

Mrs Hemmings at first didn't like the idea of other staff appearing in her kitchen without warning but she soon realized his reasons. After a mild admonishment to us both, she virtually turned a blind eye; after all Peter could whisper into Sir Samuel's ear anytime.

Our conversation was always cheerful and proper. Then one day when he thought nobody was watching he held my hand. My knees went weak.

To see more of each other we took to meeting in the market on some excuse or other. On one expedition I introduced him to my mother. He was full of charm to her and mother gave me a knowing smile. On another occasion we met Alan, the charm didn't seem to work on him. Later, while Peter was distracted, Alan whispered to me, "Beware, I know about his sort. He is not for you".

I found that rather daunting. Alan had always been concerned about me. Was he jealous or did Peter have ill intent towards me? Peter was a cut above most men; he was literate, articulate, knowledgeable. He could make me laugh and feel good, he lifted my self-esteem. Why turn away from him when everything was going so well? We progressed to lunch together and the goodbye kiss, which got better each time. It was not long before everyone seemed to notice and seemed to accept that we were interested in each other.

The first time out openly together was to the fair that arrived in Indian Queens. We enjoyed being together; for me it was the best day for years if not for ever. We talked and laughed a lot. He was intelligent, he knew all sorts of people, and had been to all sorts of places I had never heard of in his travels with Sir Samuel. He was a gentleman's gentleman. Whatever did he want with an ignorant servant girl like me? Surely a ladies' maid or some such type would be more suitable for him. It made me hang onto his arm all the more. I didn't want to lose him whatever his intentions. He was the nicest man I had come across. He was never improper or made an improper advance; if he did, I realized I would have trouble in resisting him. We spent more time together and the goodbye kiss had become more ardent. We could not get anywhere near the time we wanted together: I was busy in the kitchen for long hours and he was at the beck and call of Sir Samuel.

Seeing me with Peter set off young men on the estate to try their hand at chatting me up. Until Peter had arrived they had looked at me as a kitchen skivvy under the watchful eye of Mrs Hemmings, now they saw me as a desirable young women. None got nearer than a whispered suggestion. It all went to boost my self-esteem and make me look and feel healthier and happier.

"Don't set your sights too high," was the advice from Mrs Hemmings. "If you do and he decides to go off with some other lady you will be badly hurt."

It was all pessimistic warnings.

Then the following year there was a lot of excitement at the Manor.

Sir Samuel was going to an important meeting somewhere. He would be taking his squire, valet, groom and at least a couple of men at arms. At first I was depressed by this news. Peter would be away possibly for several weeks. Travelling to exotic places he could easily find a more suitable female. He had made no commitment to me. Then to my great surprise Mister Hemmings informed me that I would be going with them in the capacity of cook and laundry woman. When it sank in I was elated. I would be with Peter and away from Mrs Hemmings' prying eyes. Then came the worry about travelling to strange places in the company of virtual strangers.

"It will be a great chance for you to see more of the world," declared Mister Hemmings. Who had suggested my name, I wondered.

Then came the preparation and rumours of our destination. It all sounded very interesting.

"How long will we be away?" I asked Peter.

"Nobody knows, it depends on circumstances. There is much agitation in the land about who should be Regent. It could get nasty. If all goes well we should be back in about two weeks, otherwise it is anybody's guess."

"Where are we going?"

"Salisbury."

"How far is that?"

"Best part of a week to get there. We could spend time in tents so come with warm clothing."

It was with a mixture of apprehension and anticipation that we set off behind Sir Samuel on the ordained day.

I was not the only female in the group. Sir Samuel's sister, Pamela, was there and the wife of his groom, who said she would keep an eye out for me.

There were two wagons to carry supplies and tents, which meant two wagon drivers as well as the party. I sat on the tailgate of the supply wagon, which was at the end of the line. Although it was rather bumpy I could see the countryside better.

The first day took us to Bodmin. Sir Samuel stayed in the Manor of a friend while the rest of us lower orders stayed in a nearby Abbey. This meant I had no cooking duties that evening. Peter was in the Manor with the master.

The second day was a dreadful journey across Bodmin Moor. The wagons bumped and bounced along through ruts and potholes.

Much of the way I got out and walked. The rain showers on this day did not help. I had never seen a more desolate place.

Peter came back several times to see if all was well with me. Good job I was a fit young woman. We stopped by a river soon after noon in a secluded spot, a fire was lit and I skinned and cooked some rabbits that the men had caught. The groom's wife helped out. Then we were off again.

As dusk was starting to fall we came in sight of our destination for the day, Launceston Castle.

I had never seen such a place before though of course I had heard about them. Peter came along later in the evening after we had all eaten a substantial meal.

"I hope the roads are not like this all the way to Salisbury or I shall be a wreck before much longer," I said to him.

"No, the worst is over."

At least we found a quiet corner where we could have a warm embrace and a stolen kiss or two.

I slept well that night on the scullery floor with two or three other women, their chatter did not disturb me.

Next day we proceeded into Devon according to Peter, across a stone bridge over the River Tamar. On this day Peter joined me for a while on the tailgate. He was good company and made me laugh. Being in the last wagon and unseen by the others he could be playful and romantic. We ate at a roadside tavern at about noon then pressed on to Okehampton Castle on the edge of Dartmoor. It was already getting dark as we passed through the castle gates. Peter was called away immediately so we got no time together.

The next day it was pouring with rain so we got permission to stay another day. There was not a lot to do so Peter and I had time together.

I now made the decision to lead Peter on and get him committed to me. On a walk through an isolated part of the castle I became amorous with him and when he started to take liberties I took my time in stopping him. Then I swiftly tripped away leaving him eager for more at the first chance. I was playing with fire I knew, but nothing ventured, nothing gained.

The next morning, when we were ready for the off, Peter came over for a chat. The groom's wife commented on it when he was gone.

"Watch that young man, he is getting ideas."

"About what?" I asked in feigned innocence.

She did not elaborate.

This day we crossed the top of Dartmoor, another bleak and windy place.

"I thought you said we were past the rough bit?" I said to Peter when he came along.

"Ah it's the rain," he said limply. He climbed on the tailboard with me and tried to embrace me for a kiss but the bouncing and swaying thwarted him.

Sir Samuel and his sister with two armed men now rode ahead leaving the rest of us to struggle along the road as best as we could. At dusk we arrived at a place called Cheriton Bishop where Sir Samuel and those who counted were lodged in the manor house of a friend. The other men slept in a barn while the groom's wife and I slept on the kitchen floor. Peter was not encouraged to come and see me.

However we did meet in the yard and found a gloomy corner where we could embrace each other. He kissed me ardently and took liberties. I knew I was safe because too many people were about. By the time I slipped away he was definitely aroused.

The next day was another long, bumping, jolting trip that brought us to the biggest city I have ever seen.

Exeter.

It was a place full of several thousand people, an incredible number to my mind. It was surrounded by a great stone wall. The castle we stayed in that night was the biggest building I have ever been in. There were chambers and passages everywhere. I was allocated a place in a dormitory for female servants. It gave me a chance to have a chat with a new set of people about all sorts of things but mainly about men.

Peter was much in demand with Sir Samuel so by the time he found me we only had time for a quick word.

After Exeter, all the other places we stayed at or passed by were insignificant. It took longer to reach our destination than Peter told me it would, in fact it was several days after leaving Exeter that we arrived at the final destination.

During these days, Peter would often seek me out and get frisky if he could get the chance, which was not often. I gave way to his advances little by little.

As we approached Salisbury there seemed to be a lot of knights and armed men about, and I began to fear that we might get into something nasty. Peter had told me of the animosity amongst the aristocracy about who should control the infant King. The animosity had sometimes led to blows as well as legal and political controversy.

We camped outside Salisbury at a place called Britford on the banks of the river Avon. I did not have time now to worry about the squabbles of the aristocracy. I was kept busy preparing and cooking meals, washing up, and doing everybody's laundry from Indian Queens.

Sir Samuel and his sister were in Salisbury and much of the time Peter was there also. Most people slept in tents but I slept in the supply wagon.

Quite often at night there would be singing and shouting until late for there were a lot of high-spirited young men about. After dark I would slip away and climb into the wagon and lay there quietly hoping nobody knew my whereabouts.

We were there for over a week and I hardly saw Peter. Then we were told matters were settled and we were going home to Indian Queens. We stayed on for an extra day because the master wanted to take part in a tournament. I would have thought that what happened to his father would have put him off.

Most of us went to watch. I left the cooking to individuals. I had done enough in the past week and wanted to be with Peter. I spent most of the day on his arm. It was an exciting day with much to see. We all enjoyed ourselves and only one knight was killed. Peter walked me back to our camp at nightfall.

There were not many people about so we started kissing and cuddling against the wagon.

"It's getting chilly; why don't we get inside the wagon?"

His intentions were obvious. I remembered what Alan had said, not to mention mother and Mrs Hemmings.

"No we mustn't. I have a long day tomorrow."

"Oh come on, just for a little while." His hand was moving onto my crotch, then he began pulling my skirt up.

"Stop it!"

"Why? You like it."

"I'm not that sort of girl."

His hand was now on the bare flesh of my thigh and still moving up, he was kissing me more urgently than ever before. I silently prayed for help in resisting this delightful assault. I must not give way.

I left it until his hand reached what he was seeking then I jumped away.

"Somebody is coming!" The age-old cry of a young woman in a compromising situation. We stood quiet for a while, then he started again.

"You would not like somebody to do this to the woman you are going to marry, would you?" That seemed to slow him down. "I don't want to be damaged before Mister Right comes along."

"Are you saying you don't want to make love with me?"

"Why should I if you are not going to marry me. What would happen to me if I got pregnant?" I rubbed myself against him gently to keep him interested.

"Married!" It was as though he had never heard the word before.

"The man that I shall marry will have a virgin bride and be well fed."

"I'm sure he will."

He was getting quite worked up again as I continued to gently rub myself against him. Then I abruptly pulled away and called to a non-existent figure in the gloom. We still held hands in the dark.

"You will have to go."

That was too much for him.

"What would you say if I said I wanted to marry you?"

I put my arms around his neck.

"We shall have to wait and see. It is late, think about it then come back in the morning in the cold light of day and ask me."

I pulled away and went to join the groom and his wife who had just appeared. Peter did not follow.

I went to bed late but could not sleep. I had dragged things out into the open between us. Would he come back or be scared off?

Chapter Ten

Next morning we were all busy packing and getting back on the road to Indian Queens. Perhaps it was a good chance for Peter to avoid me.

The start of the journey was like a carnival: everybody waving at each other and calling out as we all moved out. Whether the conference was any cause for joy, I did not know.

I scanned the column for Peter but he was nowhere, neither was the master. No news is good news but only in some cases.

Drizzle began as we turned on the road to the west. As we went along with no sign of Peter, I got more miserable. I had not let him have his way last night, now he was gone. We stopped for a break in the early afternoon and there he was with a smile on his face.

I had to restrain myself from rushing up to him but he came straight to me.

"Can we have a quiet word somewhere?"

"Of course."

We moved off together round the back of the wagon out of sight of our companions. My heart was thumping madly; was this good news or bad?

"Mary I think we have known each other long enough. You know how I feel about you." There was a pause as he took my hand and looked me straight in the eye. "Mary will you marry me?"

My ears did not seem to catch it, or perhaps the brain could not comprehend it. Perhaps I was getting over emotional and hearing things. I wanted to be sure.

"Pardon?"

"Will you marry me?"

There was no mistake or confusion this time.

I flung my arms around his neck and kissed him on the lips.

"Of course darling," I said joyfully.

We kissed and embraced a little longer, then still holding hands and with a big smile.

"We shall have to see your parents first and Sir Samuel before we tell anyone else."

"I don't need anybody's permission. I am twenty years old and my parents, as you call them, are not really: my mother died when I was born."

"Well it would be courteous to ask them, and Sir Samuel will expect to be told first. I am his valet and he might take a dim view if he heard second-hand."

"Will you tell him now?"

"No, the time is not right. I will give a hint or two then speak openly when we are back at the Manor."

"Well don't leave it too long my darling."

How was I supposed to contain myself and not tell anybody on the journey home? I did not know, but I did. I was very happy and Peter was a fine catch. The groom's wife suspected and hinted but asked nothing.

Though he came round several evenings and during the day, I decided to keep my legs closed until all was in the open. It boosted my confidence and made him more eager. The journey home was worse than the one out, for the weather was worse and the roads muddier and more rutted. More than once the wagons got stuck and the men had to give a hand to get things moving. Then near Bodmin a wheel broke, and we had several hours delay before it was put right.

We were all grateful when we clattered in to Indian Queens. If that was what the rest of the world looked like I would stay at Indian Queens.

The first night back I slept like a log and had to be shaken awake. There was work to be done.

I saw Peter at dinner and he said he had not had a chance to speak to Sir Samuel yet. I had a nasty thought that he might say nothing until he had his way with me. After all there were no witnesses so he could change his mind. So I was a little sharp with him.

That afternoon he came back with a big smile. After the intervention of Pamela, Sir Samuel had approved the idea of our marriage. They both wanted to see us for a chat tomorrow evening. I discreetly told Mrs Hemmings, which seemed to please her, then got permission to take my intended to meet my parents for their approval; by evening it would all be over the Manor.

Mother was well pleased. Father came in from the pig sty and was also well pleased with me. I shuddered to think what Peter thought of him, he was dirty, smelly and unshaven. Peter turned not a hair.

Before we returned to the Manor mother gave me some bad news. Alan's wife had lost her baby at birth; this was the second time.

The following evening we were conducted by Mister Hemmings to see Sir Samuel with his two sisters Pamela and Joan present. Women love to hear about a wedding. They did try to put me at ease and chatted about my future. I was handed a glass of French wine. I was petrified.

"Well we shall have to re-arrange your living accommodation won't we. Bring Mrs Jones in," said Sir Samuel. I left most of the talking to Peter. While the two girls were talking to the housekeeper Sir Samuel moved close up and in a low voice asked, "You are not pregnant are you girl?"

I blushed terribly at such a question which was going to be asked often in the next few weeks.

"Oh no sir!"

"So there is no mad rush then."

"I think they ought to get it over with; we do have a spare room they can have," said Pamela coming back from speaking to Mrs Jones.

Then Joan piped up.

"Perhaps they won't want to stay here once they are married."

We both quickly denied this.

Sir Samuel showed mild concern that with Peter sleeping in a different part of the house it might interfere with his duties as his valet.

Pamela scotched that doubt.

Sir Samuel for a lark then asked if he could claim the first night as lord of the manor. He was immediately rebuked by everyone.

"Good old customs are dying out everywhere," he said in mock gloom.

So we were accepted and they picked the date, 22th Aug 1428.

When I returned to the kitchen Mrs Hemmings also asked the question and was greatly relieved.

I was concerned to have things right for the day. People now gave us more time and room together. Peter still pressed to have his way with me, more so now we were committed to being married. I was terrified of falling pregnant too soon. We got into several heated clinches where Peter got more than I thought he was entitled to without getting it all. He certainly gave me more thrills than I had ever had before. I wondered if I would make it to the altar intact, but the fear of pregnancy compelled me to stop him before things went too far.

Two days before the wedding a small boy appeared at the kitchen door from the village.

Mrs Hemmings answered his knock.

"Please Missus, Mistress Mills wants to know if her daughter can come down to the farm, she says it's important."

"Not yet she can't! She is busy."

I overheard the conversation and snatched the door wide open.

"Is something wrong?" Mother had never sent for me before while I had been at the Manor.

"Not that I know of," said the boy.

"She will come later when she has finished her work!" Mrs Hemmings shut the door in the boy's face.

"Just get on with your work!" She had not been so brusque for a long time.

Within an hour she had mellowed and her husband intervened.

"Get off with you but don't take all day!"

So I hurried straight down to the farm and went in.

"Ah my dear, I want you to meet somebody."

Had she got me out of the Manor just to meet a stranger? Surely not.

A man across the room that I had not noticed stood up and came towards us. An elderly man in his fifties, well-built but shabbily dressed.

"Mary, I want you to meet your real father."

I was speechless. He took me in strong arms and hugged me. I saw tears rolling down his cheeks which set me off. We all got quite emotional.

Mother had somehow got word to him and he had come down to see me married.

Edith's husband came in and it felt strange to have two fathers in the same room. Conversation once begun rolled relentlessly with questions on both sides.

Father stayed at the farm until after the wedding then he slipped away as quietly as he had come.

So on the 22nd of Aug 1428 I became Mistress Jenkins, I gave my maiden name as Mills. At first I found physical love both painful and embarrassing but he was happy and that is what counted with me. Very soon the pain and embarrassment went and we both enjoyed ourselves. I felt a little guilty over this because I had been told women do these things out of duty not pleasure.

I was very soon pregnant and as happy as could be.

The year of 1429 was a year to remember for a number of reasons.

First Mrs Hemmings died one night without warning. This caused confusion and I had to take charge of the kitchen on the spot. Mister Hemmings was unhinged and unable to attend to his duties with any degree of competence.

Then the master came home with a new wife.

She began to organise the staff right away. Mister Hemmings would have to pull himself together right now or go. Her husband did not need a valet. With the housekeeper she interviewed a couple of women for the post of cook, then I was offered the post. My reply was blunter then they expected.

"I am a married woman, if you say my husband must go then so shall I!"

The new Lady was a bossy cow but this brought her to a standstill. Mrs Jones started to raise her voice against me but the mistress silenced her. Then after a moment's thought I was dismissed back to the kitchen. The upshot was that Peter was offered the job of butler in place of Mister Hemmings who would have to go. I would have the job of chief cook and also the vacated room of the Hemmings.

So all round a lot of people were not happy. I didn't want the responsibility of head cook to such a large household in the last stages of my first pregnancy. Peter didn't want the job of butler, Mister Hemmings was rendered unemployed and homeless, the housekeeper got a new domineering boss, and the master had lost his valet. I heard that Pamela and Joan were not too happy with the new set up. It goes to show that new brooms can sweep chaos.

There was one more upheaval before my baby was born. Father sold his land and became the inn keeper at The King Alfred in town.

Mother was not happy at all. I gave birth to a fine, healthy son whom we called John. Within two days I was back in the kitchen.

One good thing the new mistress did was to establish a nursery for all the children of the staff, for there were several running about. My son was too little so I kept him in a drawer near me while I was working; a nursery would be ideal when he started to run about. I could not have him near the kitchen stoves.

After John was born things began to change between Peter and I. With the attention that the baby required he felt neglected. He became jealous and moody, at the same time he did not like his new job and wasn't very good at it, he felt beholden to me for keeping him at the Manor which didn't do his ego much good. He had been happy as a valet, as butler there was much to do and too many people he had to control.

When he came to me for comfort and support, I was too busy with our son to pay much attention. I realized then that he was a weak man who did not think positively. Up to now his life had been easy. Peter liked to be the centre of attention and subconsciously resented his son's intrusion. Friction began between us. He got very annoyed if the baby cried in the night, then I got annoyed with him.

Trying to put things right between us resulted in another baby, a daughter. With a full time job and two babies to look after I could give Peter even less attention.

I noticed as John grew bigger so did the resentment; this did not apply to our daughter. Peter took to her right away and she could do no wrong in Peter's eyes. This upset me. I loved both my children. I could not do much about Peter's attitude so we became even more estranged.

Then the Mistress fell pregnant which set off a lot of gossip and also took much of the fire out of the Mistress for a time.

On occasion I would escape the Manor on business in the market. Here I met Alan again. He was very depressed at the time because his wife had lost her third child at birth. Joan was not a very healthy woman at all. He talked quite a bit about Joan as we walked round the market. Father was doing alright at his inn, in fact he was enjoying it, and mother had come round to accepting and liking her new life. Alan would also tell me news from afar. Some French witch by the name of Joan had brought about an English defeat at a place called Orleans. The widow of Henry the Fifth had married a commoner by the name of Tudor when she could have had the Duke of Somerset. These things did not interest me but he felt the need to tell people what he knew. Because he always listened to me in childhood so I now listened to him. I needed somebody also that I could talk to about my crumbling marriage but I said nothing.

We took to having lunch together once a month at the King Alfred, where I could see mother. Father would not accept payment. Alan did not tell Joan that we met like this. Why? It was all innocent family and general talk. Or was it?

For me the joy of being married to Peter was tarnished as he became more sarcastic, critical and threatening. There was no joy for me in bed with him: he had his way and I lay still. Sometimes I cried afterwards for the love that we had lost. I soon fell pregnant again and life became even more of a drudge. We called the child Kathleen and Peter was pleased with her but he became harder with John who was now three years old. I tried to protect my son as much as possible, which annoyed Peter more than ever and led to the first physical attack on me. It was not the last. I tried to hide the tears, especially from the children. I tried to get John to sleep in the evenings before his father appeared but it was not always possible. The nice little room we had taken over from the Hemmings was now cluttered and noisy with five of us living in it.

Peter would smack John for any reason or none, he would belittle him or try to set Mary against him. He never smacked any of the girls or spoke harshly to them. I was becoming increasingly depressed and the blows and abuse from Peter increased. Two years after Kathleen I gave birth to another daughter, Joan.

Being pregnant and with three small children was not a good set up especially when holding down a responsible job. During the day the eldest was now in the nursery but in the evenings we were all together in our little room and there was always one that was fractious.

Alan noticed something was wrong and that I was not very well. So as in the days gone by I leaned on his shoulder and let it all flow out. Whether he spoke to mother or not I didn't know but mother turned up and mentioned that I looked run down. She offered to take my two girls away for a while in the last stages of my pregnancy. I persuaded her to take John and Kathleen.

From there on Peter seemed happier but I was not happy without my little boy, although he was in good hands and it was not permanent. With John gone Peter's conduct towards me improved, he hit me less often and was less abusive.

During the worst times he never was nasty when people were about or left bruises where they did show.

John was happy with his grandparents and I let him stay while Joan was an infant. I thought that when Joan was on her feet I would take John and Kathleen back, but time dragged on. I didn't want John exposed to Peter's aggression again. The months became years.

Alan now worked in the inn and, when John was seven years old, father gave him a permanent job. Going down to see my son also brought me into contact with Alan. One day when Alan and I were alone he surprised me.

"Why don't you leave Peter and the Manor. I'm sure dad could find you a job here. You will be happier and better off."

"I can't do that! Mum and Dad would never approve of me walking out on my husband. I would never hold my head up again." I was shocked at his suggestion. "My place is with my husband!"

"Your place is where you are happy and secure."

"Leave it alone. I should not have told you how things were." With that I left quickly.

In the year 1440 father died suddenly and Alan took over the inn. Joan moved in with him. Alan kept John at the inn.

The following year mother, who could not get over father's death, died herself, followed rather quickly by Joan who had never been very fit. Things go in threes they say.

Alan was left a widow at thirty-eight years of age. Things soon began to look different.

Chapter Eleven

The fact that I knew Alan would need a shoulder to cry on and I wanted to see more of my growing son led me to taking time off from my kitchen duties. I had a competent assistant who wanted to do more so I let her.

Not only did Alan find time to confide in me but after a couple of months when we had had a longish chat about old days he kissed me. At first it was only a peck but it soon flowered into a warm, loving kiss. We were back where we were twenty years ago. It confused me but it was very pleasant and set my heart thumping like it had not done for a long time. If Alan felt better for a kiss and a mild flirtation then why not; it need not go further. After all, I was a married woman with children. Things between Peter and I might not be perfect but he was my husband for whom I was required to forsake all others.

Soon after this, Peter got ideas. He insisted that his two children should return from the King Alfred and live with us at the Manor. This was sparked off by Mary becoming a house maid and moving to a different part of the Manor, up into the attic to be precise. Peter suddenly felt he was losing his children; only Joan was with us.

"John cannot come back here. He works at the King Alfred."

"Only with that brother of yours."

"No matter who he works for, he contributes towards his own keep while he is there. What would he do here and where would he sleep?"

"Here of course, in our room."

"I think not. He is a lad of thirteen. The Mistress and Mrs Jones might object and the boy has to earn his keep."

"They are my children!"

"John is working at the King Alfred."

"What about Kathleen?"

Now that had me stumped, but at least I could not see Kathleen antagonising her father like John did just by being.

"I'll go and fetch her myself!" With that he stamped out of the room.

Joan thought the return of a big sister was great, having lost the eldest up those mysterious stairs. At ten years of age it was past time for Kathleen to be working, she had had it easy up to now. After a word with Mrs Jones who had a word with the Mistress, Kathleen was employed with me in the kitchen as a maid. Another good thing was that she and Joan were given a little bedroom of their own. Peter and I were together alone at last.

Peter liked this arrangement and though he still didn't like being a butler he stopped all his complaining and we began to get on better. We had both organised and eased our work load so that we were not tired and snapping at each other when we met.

I still went to the King Alfred to see our son and Alan. Peter was well aware but why should he object to a sister keeping an eye on a widowed brother? He also began to ask how John was getting on.

Being on his own even though he had the inn to run was getting at Alan, he was not used to it.

"If you want to give up work at the Manor I could employ you as a cook. You could live in."

"Oh, and what about the present cook?"

"I would get rid of her, she is not much good as a cook and she comes in late quite often. I would get rid of her on the spot if you want the job."

"What about Peter?"

"I'm sure I could fit him in somewhere if you want him. He will be happier here than with that snotty lot."

"You two would never get on under the same roof. Look at the shouting match you two had over Kathleen."

"That is water under the bridge."

"That might be so but Peter wouldn't take to you giving him orders. So I think you had better forget the idea."

"Very well. But the offer for you is still open."

As if to persuade me he gave me a more ardent kiss and cuddle before I left. It boosted my ego and left me feeling that I was in control as well as giving me a romantic fillip. Life was getting better. There was also a delicious feeling of guilt.

It was a little while after that when I went down to the King Alfred that Alan took me into an alcove in the Bar Room. There were people about so I was not concerned about his motives; he seemed rather serious.

"Mary, my dear do you believe in life after death and reincarnation?"

What an odd question to ask at this time of day and this place.

"After death you will go to Heaven or Hell according to your merits. Any priest will tell you that." Whatever was he getting at?

"I am not concerned with what priests say."

"Alan, I don't know what you are talking about but perhaps you ought to go to church more often."

"I hardly ever go these days, I have an inn to run. For a long time I have felt they are not telling all the truth."

"Whatever do you mean?"

"I mean the destination of our souls."

"Have you been talking to some Lollards? If so you could get yourself into serious trouble."

"No I haven't. I don't know any."

"They don't carry a flag. They will get at you without warning or identification. Whoever has been getting at you, you should expose him now for the good of your own soul; not to mention what could happen if you get involved."

"Mary, listen to me. You are the only one I can tell this to."

"You could talk to Father Ripon."

"He would not understand. Just give me five minutes, Mary please."

"Very well Alan but don't be surprised if I don't believe what you say."

"It is difficult to speak of what I know." He looked around the room. Nobody was paying us any attention; we were just brother and sister having a chat.

"Do you believe in the immortal soul within us all?"

"Yes of course."

"The soul is not for one life, it is on going. What you do wrong in this life you will have to put right in the next. You do not go into a fiery pit. If you do wrong to somebody you will come back as a victim."

"That sounds like justice."

"It's more. We have to improve our souls over several lives so that we can move to a higher plane of existence. In doing so we are often with the same people as our soul goes on its journey. It is called reincarnation. You can look back in time that is called regression."

"Well it sounds interesting."

"This is not the first time we have been here on this earth together."

I found I was willing to listen to this new theory on life.

"You are saying we lived together in this world before?"

"Yes."

"When?"

"About eighty years ago we were lovers in France."

Ah, so that was what it was all about. It was certainly the best chat up line I had ever heard of.

"I'm sorry Alan I must go." I caught the eye of John and stood up as he approached. I kissed Alan on the cheek.

"Goodbye."

"Think of what I have said, Mary," he said as he held my hand.

"Yes dear." I took John's arm and walked to the door.

For the rest of the week what Alan had said stayed on my mind. Was Alan losing his marbles? Was he trying to seduce me? Had he found something about life that nobody else knew. Was he under the influence of the Lollards? I had never heard the word reincarnation before; could he have made that up?

It was longer than normal before I went down to the King Alfred again, but go I did. Again, against my will, or was it? Alan and I ended up in an alcove, only this time we could not be seen and we could not see anybody unless they came very close.

"Have you thought about what I said last time?"

"You mean about having more than one life?"

"Yes."

"It sounds weird. I think you should leave that thing alone."

"Once you know truth you cannot leave it alone."

"Who told you these things?"

"Nobody told me anything. Joan and her sister set me thinking so I thought I would find out."

"So you just sat down and off the top of your head decided we were lovers eighty years ago."

"No, I found out how I can go back in time."

"I think one life is enough for anyone. Who was I supposed to be in the last life?"

"Thomas Simon, an archer on campaign in France. We met at Calais. I was a French woman by the name of Isobel Jaifrok."

"Did we get married?"

"No but we had two children."

"Did we indeed." Was he having delusions or just winding me up?

"Do you have strange dreams, Alan?"

"No."

"Was there just you and me there."

"No, your husband Peter was there. He was your wife then."

That was too much and I made an excuse to leave.

Should I tell somebody that Alan was no longer himself. Who, without causing trouble? There was nothing sinister in it; or was there?"

I took the plunge with Peter when he was in a mellow mood.

"Peter do you believe that people can come back to life as somebody else after they have died?"

He burst out laughing.

"A load of nonsense. Reincarnation they call it. I've heard of it. Why? Has somebody been telling you stories of lost souls wandering through the centuries?"

"No. I just heard it mentioned the other day in the market and was curious."

"If it were true the priest would have told us."

"Yes, I suppose so."

The next time I saw Alan I decided I would put him on the spot.

When next I went down to the King Alfred it was I who led the way to a secluded alcove.

"Alan, if nobody told you about reincarnation how did you find out? How do you know I was Thomas Simon? Tell me."

"Joan's sister had this pendulum which some gypsy had given her. Handled correctly it can tell your past life and future. He told her how to use it but she was too frightened to do so. She was going to throw it away several times. She did tell me how to use it so when she died I took it. I tried it out recently just like the gypsy said. I was astounded at the results. I had to tell someone and you were the only person I could think of."

We were silent for a while.

"What did Joan say about it?"

131

"I never used it while she was alive, though she knew I had it. Like her sister she was frightened of it."

"Where is this pendulum now?"

"Upstairs in a wooden box. Do you want to come and see it?"

"If I went up to your bedroom now Alan, your staff and your customers would see us and talk would fly around. They would get all sorts of ideas."

We sat quietly for a moment.

"You think I am after you, don't you Mary?"

"Yes."

"Well I am fond of you Mary but I don't want to cause you any trouble or embarrassment. We have always had a soft spot for each other I think it is to do with our past lives."

"Well next time I come I want to see this pendulum of yours."

We changed the subject and chatted away for a while, then when it was time to go he kissed me ardently and I responded. I found it strangely hard to leave him and go home.

Next time I did not leave it so long before going down to the King Alfred. After chatting as usual to my son and others, Alan drew me away to our alcove. This time before anything was said he took me in his arms and gave me a long lustful kiss, it really made my heart flutter.

"Behave, before somebody catches us!"

We came apart but still held hands out of sight.

"Now Alan, what about this pendulum of yours or did you make it all up to get me in your bedroom?"

"I have it here."

He drew out a small wooden box and opened the lid, inside was what appeared to be a necklace about eight inches long. On the end of it was a small crystal pendant. I reached forward to pick it out but Alan stopped me.

"Like a dog, it has only one owner." He plucked it out and dangled it before me.

"Are you saying this thing has magic powers?"

"I know it has."

"Show me!"

"It doesn't work like that. Ask me a question to which I cannot possibly have the answer and next time you come I will tell you the answer."

132

"How would you find the answer?"

"I hold the pendulum pointing down and ask a question and it answers. Never failed yet."

"Weird."

"I call it fantastic."

"Some people would call it witchcraft. Hide it away and say nothing to nobody or you could be in very serious trouble."

"I have told nobody but you. Now what is your question?"

"I don't know but I will think of something."

I did think about it all the time. A pendulum that answers questions. Which of us was mad. If it was witchcraft the Devil would be involved. Should I tell the priest? My mind was in turmoil. Peter noticed it and thought I was sickening for something and became attentive which was unusual for him.

A question to which Alan could not know the answer? That was the problem I had to put my mind to to break the power of his pendulum.

Then the answer was there before me.

The Mistress had an elder sister who popped in on a visit from far away. I gleaned all the information about her that I could from Mrs Jones, Peter and Mary. Then I was ready.

Off I went to the King Alfred on market day to put Alan and his pendulum to the test. The inn was very busy and it was some time before Alan was free to sit with me in the alcove.

"Do you still want me to give you obscure questions?" I asked him after he had kissed me more ardently than a man would kiss his sister.

"Fire away."

"Right. The Lady Turner has an older sister. What is her christian name and her maiden name? What is her husband's christian name. How many children have they and what are their ages?"

"That is one question is it?"

"If your pendulum is any good it will romp through."

"Well as you can see we are a bit pushed. I will have the answers next week."

"No! I want the answers before I leave here." Giving him until next week would give him the chance to ask around.

"I don't know if I have the time."

"You have time to sit here and talk to me. You are the boss here, you can disappear if you want." He was pinned down.

"Alright." He stood up and went and spoke to one of his staff then went upstairs. It seemed a long time before he came back. Sitting on my own invited various strangers in town for the market to give me an inquisitive glance to see if I was up for grabs like some other women in the inn. One tried his luck and was sent packing. Alan at last returned and sat close to me.

"The sister's name is Isobel, her maiden name was Walker, her husband's name is Gilbert. They have two children, girls aged three and five." He could see my surprise. "As a bonus Peter will out live you by six years."

That made my mouth drop open.

"Does that satisfy you or do you have more questions?"

I could not answer.

"Well Mary you think on it but say nothing. I must go now." He kissed me on the lips and was gone.

I was in even more turmoil than before.

Next time I met him he had more spare time.

"Tell me Alan about these previous lives of ours."

"Ah, yes. You were Thomas Simon from a place called Papworth Everard. You served as an archer with King Edward at the battle of Crecy. We met soon after at Calais and became lovers. I was a widow and you were married to your first wife."

"Now that was naughty," I said and snuggled closer with a grin.

"It was wartime and you had been away from your wife a long time."

"Did you say we had two children?"

"Yes."

"How long have you known all this?"

"About a month. Remember how attracted to each other we were soon as we knew we were not brother and sister?"

"Yes. Left alone we might have become lovers again." The thought gave me a warm feeling.

"Next time you come on a non-market day, we can have lunch in my room and have a long talk more privately."

"That would be nice."

I found during the week as I waited for the day to come round that I was strangely excited at the thought of more privacy with Alan.

Would it be safe, for he was into witchcraft. Never mind, Alan would do me no harm and I might find out more about these strange powers he had discovered.

I told Peter I would have lunch with Alan and he thought it was a nice idea which might cheer me up. Nobody said anything about me being away from the Manor more often.

I felt I was entering a new phase of my life.

Chapter Twelve

I saw my son before I went openly up the stairs and into Alan's bedroom. A table was already laid out. Soon after we arrived a servant brought in hot food to be set before us. Alan told the servant he did not wish to be disturbed, to make sure he put a sign on the door.

His bed was in the corner, a chest nearby, and under the window a small desk with quills and parchment. Where and when did he learn to write? The room was not large but it was cosy.

We started to eat and pass the usual pleasantries as though we were a normal man and wife. It was when we came to the bread and cheese that he raised the subject of reincarnation and his magic pendulum.

"Do you now believe in reincarnation after what I have told you?"

"No. I think is it something to do with witchcraft."

"It is not. I am willing to answer any questions you have."

"It is still witchcraft and you can get into very serious trouble. I think you ought to drop that pendulum down some dark hole."

"No way. We have found a strange magic access to some very interesting information. It makes sense of life. Reincarnation and Karma is based on justice and the progress of the soul."

"What happens to those who live a blameless life? Will they not enter Heaven? Must we all keep going round?"

"We cannot perfect our souls in one life time. Once we have passed all the tests and hurdles then we shall go to a higher plane of existence."

"What about those who never get it right? Do they go round forever?"

"That is why we reincarnate together with people we know so that we can help each other."

"Is that so? Who else have I lived with before, beside you and Peter?"

"In a previous life our mother was your sister, father was your first wife in your last life. Robert Stephen our cousin was your eldest son John. Your present son was your daughter-in-law Joan Hill."

"Enough! Enough! You make my head spin."

Alan was quiet for a while, then he poured more wine and stood up.

"Come and sit over here with me."

So we got up from the hard chairs and went to sit on the edge of his bed.

"Does it all confuse you?"

"Yes."

"Well I was like that when it first began but the information built up so fast just for the asking that I had no option but to believe. I want to share this knowledge with you, Mary."

We put our goblets down and embraced. It was a close and loving embrace ending with a warm kiss.

"Will we live again do you think?"

"I don't have to think, I know."

"Where will it all end?" I clung a little closer to him. Was it the wine that was making me receptive to him? Or was it the magic story he told? Was it the memories of twenty years ago when he was always my protector?

"Be not afraid Mary. I shall always be here for you."

I knew that was true and snuggled closer, I wanted to hear more of this magic story. This seemed to do something to him, he kissed me with a demanding passion. I responded with enthusiasm. I was tingling all over and welcomed his wandering hands. I laid back on the bed and grasped his head as his gentle fingers moved up my skirt to my bare thighs stroking and caressing me, not like Peter's demanding grasp. We kissed with a growing passion for we knew we were meant for each other. He moved to get himself into a better position to have his way with me. Alarm bells rang.

"Get off! Somebody is coming!"

We came apart and sat up. This was not right, I was a married woman. I had a son in the building. It was sinful to go further. The thought of being caught in the act and being labelled a whore and adulterer made me go cold.

"Come, we must go before somebody comes looking."

137

He tried to pull me down again for he was, as I saw, fully roused. An impish thought came to me. I leaned over and kissed him and ran my fingers down to that tempting bulge. A stroke and a squeeze and it was all over for him. I broke away and jumped up with a gleeful chuckle. I had given Alan pleasure but I had not committed the sin of adultery.

"We must go!"

"I suppose so." He heaved himself up and gave me a gentle kiss.

"Thank you for coming, Mary. Will you come to dinner again next week?"

"Only if you behave yourself, you naughty man."

We grinned at each other as he opened the door and escorted me down to the porch. I felt exhilarated for the rest of the day. Only when all was quiet in the night did the things that Alan had said came back to fill my head. Whatever was it all about?

A couple of days later I went down to the King Alfred ostensibly to see my son and also to thank Alan for a lovely meal, but in reality to arrange a day for our next dinner together. Alan had once more become a central figure in my life.

In less than a week, I was back in his room for a lovely meal washed down with good French wine. Over the wine the conversation became serious.

"Have you spoken to any Lollards, Alan?"

"Not to my knowledge but you meet all sorts of people when you run an inn."

"Do you know of anybody else with a pendulum like yours?"

"No, nobody. I have never heard of one before."

"Would it be possible to get the same results with any pendulum?"

"I don't know."

"Do you think we should tell Father Ripon?"

"Are you mad! If he found out there is no end to the trouble we could be in. Say nothing to nobody!"

"Come let us sit together." That cheered him up. I knew what he thought but was sure I could control the situation. We sat on the edge of the bed like last time.

"Why should the Church tell us we have only one life by which we will be judged, when your pendulum tells us there are more?"

138

"The Church wants to frighten you so it can control you and get rich and powerful. If God is so benevolent and loving why does he, according to the Church, commit so many to eternal fire?"

"In most cases a priest can intercede for you."

"What God – in charge of all the world and everything in it – has time to listen to a prattling priest? Even I haven't got time to listen to one of them."

"Alan, you are a heretic and one day you will say too much."

Secretly I was overwhelmed by the wonder of what he said. I had always been fonder of him than a cousin ought to be. How could I not snuggle up to such a clever lovely man, a man who had been my hero since I learnt to walk? I lay back on the bed with a warm inviting desire.

This time we went further than last time and I was carried away. It was Alan who called a halt, he had heard a creak on the stairs. We jumped up and straightened our clothes just as there came a knock on the door. Alan opened it and there was John who had come to see me before he went off on some task.

The three of us had a short chat then I kissed Alan on the cheek. Had John noticed the disarranged bed and our flushed faces. I had been aroused more than anytime in years. I calmed down as best as I could and followed John downstairs.

That week I was in a dreadful emotional turmoil. I went to church in the hope of guidance but there was none. When Peter made advances to me one night I repulsed him. That was unusual but more unusual was that he accepted the rebuff. In the past he would have forced himself on me, a matrimonial variation on rape.

I knew that if I continued to see Alan I would sooner or later commit adultery, then what would happen to my immortal soul? I was being drawn like a moth to the flame. I prayed.

The day arrived when I went down to the King Alfred again. The meal was not quite ready so John, Alan and I had time for a chat in the public bar. When we went up the stairs to dinner, John went off on some errand for Alan.

We had difficulty in conversation and in eating, both our minds were on the bed there in the corner inviting us over. We missed out on the bread and cheese to get there. There was only a short, disconnected conversation about magic and the Church before we got down to what had been on our minds twenty years before.

139

This time there was no stopping. He had my skirts up round my waist and was mounting me as I kissed him furiously. The penetration was mind blowing. Peter could not match this. I clung to Alan like a limpet trying to be quiet until we both reached fulfilment.

It took us time to recover and separate, we then went back to the table for more wine. A door had opened for us and would never close.

"Was it like this in Calais?"

"Yes but the roles were reversed as happens with reincarnation."

I sat down to contemplate the situation. I was now definitely a sinner and an adulteress. I was not greatly worried; to my surprise, I was no longer sceptical of what Alan said.

"It is getting late, I shall have to go."

"See you next week same day."

"I'll think about it."

"I'll be waiting."

The fact that I now had a real lover destroyed the sexual side of my marriage, for what it was worth. I was in turmoil more than ever. My whole background, never mind the Church, told me what I had done was wrong. But I knew that if I was with Alan that attitude would change. I found it difficult to look Peter in the face. Did he suspect? Should I confess at church without naming names.

Then I was back with Alan, this time there was no holding us. We ignored the food on the table and after a passionate kiss I was on my back on the bed naked for him to feast his eyes on before he gave me the satisfaction I craved. We played for a little while afterwards, he was full of complements for my body.

This could not go on, much as we would like it to. We got up, got dressed and sat down for a meal, though it had grown cold we ate it.

"This cannot go on, we are sure to be found out."

"So?"

"What do you mean by 'So'?"

"We love each other Mary, not just recently but back for at least eighty years so how can what other people think have any affect on us?"

"For a start there are laws and punishments for adulterers. You will be safe, but I won't be if it comes to light – and it will. Also I have a husband."

"None of which mean anything in the long term if we love each other, and we do."

140

"I'm thinking of the short term."

"In the short term you can move in here as cook, leave everything and come to me."

That startled me.

"Mary, the Church objects to people committing adultery here and there, not to people who live together as man and wife. Not that the Church can say much, in Exeter they run the brothels."

"Alan! What a shocking thing to say. Anyway I wasn't really thinking of the Church but its affect on my family."

"You must go where your heart dictates, Mary."

How true. Duty or love? I would have to make a decision one day but not today.

On the way home I had a feeling of contentment. I had the best of both worlds: a good job, a husband, a roof over my head and an exciting lover. My contentment was not based on sex but on the fact that Alan and I belonged to each other no matter what happened. I would never need any other shoulder to lean on.

There was the possibility that if I went to be cook at the King Alfred, Peter might follow. If not, what about Joan? She was only ten years old and not in work yet. I would have to attend to that straight away. On my return to the Manor there was another problem. The young assistant I had left in charge was not good at controlling the junior staff or in keeping unwanted people out of the kitchen. Mrs Jones was annoyed, I had to re-establish my authority. Finding a place for Joan was easy, the Mistress had already decided it was time she was at work and had obtained a place for her a couple of miles away as a kitchen maid, so that was settled without reference to what Joan or Peter thought about it. The Mistress had decided that Joan could not go on loafing about the Manor. I felt without regret that my days as a mother were over; my children would fare as well as anybody else's.

Mrs Jones hinted that I must spend more time in the kitchen or expect trouble. She insisted that my first duty was to the Turner family. Her words had the opposite effect to that intended. After missing more than a week of Alan to get things in the kitchen under control again, I wandered down again on a market day and in John's presence made a dinner date. It all looked above board. Before the day in question I spoke sternly to the kitchen staff. I also fended Peter off. I think he was beginning to suspect that I had a lover. There was no denying that I wanted to be back in Alan's arms.

141

This time both Alan and I stripped off and jumped into bed straight away. It was great! We not only made love, we explored each others' bodies with joyful abandon. Alan was better endowed than Peter. We had to force ourselves to give up on these delights. People would talk and dinner was going cold.

"I think you would be a lot better off here as cook than in that Manor House with a husband you don't love anymore. I have reserved a room for you, you can move in anytime."

"I don't know why you complain about the cook, the meals seem very good to me. On top of that you are getting forbidden fruit. Why change anything?"

"Several customers have complained."

"Well I just can't move in, though it might be nice. I have to think of other things."

"Rubbish! Happiness and welfare come first. You have no children that you are responsible for, it is time now to think of yourself. Your duty is done."

"I don't think I can forget my children just like that, and there are still the marriage vows. Now tell me about this pendulum of yours, are you going to let me handle it?"

"No, if you want one I'll see if I can get one for you."

"Does it tell you what is going to happen in this life?"

"I expect it does if you know the questions to ask."

There was a knocking at the door and John joined us for ten minutes.

I said goodbye to Alan like a fond sister should at the top of the stairs where we could be seen, then went down to the porch with John.

"Mother dear, is there anything between you and Uncle Alan?"

God it had been noticed! I stopped dead and looked at him in astonishment and panic.

"Whatever are you talking about boy? We are brother and sister."

"No you are not. Father was here the other day, from the way he talked he seemed to think that you two were having an affair. I didn't tell him that you spend over an hour in Uncle Alan's room when you come here but somebody will!"

"Your father here, asking about me?"

"Yes. But he was discreet."

"Not discreet enough by the sound of it. I shall speak very sharply to him when I get home!" I snorted indignantly, then quickly walked away before John pressed the matter like teenagers do.

I did raise the question with Peter when I got home and accused him of spying on me. My mind was in a turmoil. If husband and children suspected, what about the other people, especially the gossipy people who worked at the inn. The game was nearly up. The rules of play changed a lot quicker than I expected.

Several days later Mrs Jones said the Mistress wanted to see me right away. I thought that was odd, it was not our usual day to discuss the week's menu.

As soon as I walked in the room with Mrs Jones I knew something was wrong.

"Mrs Jenkins I have brought you here to give you a fair warning. Of late you have not been up to your normal standard; you spend too much time leaving junior staff in charge. I cannot let the standards of the senior staff slip. If you need to go out on private business, you must ask permission. Sir Samuel is a very busy person with lots of people coming to see him, which requires extra work and supervision in the kitchen. I understand that Mrs Jones has already spoken to you about your falling standards. If there is something wrong that is worrying you tell me and perhaps I can put it right. An efficient staff I will have!"

I was taken by surprise but as the criticism unrolled I became annoyed. I was not a serf. As Alan said, I had my own life to lead.

"Are you saying you are not satisfied with me?"

"With your present conduct, no!"

"In that case get yourself another cook!"

I turned on my heels and marched out the door. As I went through the door I looked back and saw the pair of them with their mouths wide open. It was a pleasure to behold. Cough on that I thought.

I did not return to the kitchen but went straight to our room and began to pack things that were essential or strictly mine, in a small bag. I collected some money out of a draw which I might need. As I packed I got angrier. I was not owned by the Turners, I didn't see why I should put up with them anymore. It was not my idea to come to the Manor in the first place.

The door opened and in walked Peter.

143

"What do you think you are doing? Put those things back and go and apologise to Lady Turner this instant!"

The fact that I was accustomed to taking orders from my husband made it very difficult for me to stand my ground but I did.

"No I won't! I am going! You are welcome to come with me or stay and be a doormat!"

He exploded.

"Are you raving mad! Walk out of here and nobody will employ you as long as you live!"

"We will see."

I picked up my bag and made for the door. He barred my way.

"I'm not letting you go anywhere. You have a duty to the Turner family and I am your husband!"

"Big deal. Now get out of my way!"

"It's that brother of yours that has put you up to this. Is that where you are going?"

"You are entitled to come with me wherever I go. It's your choice. Now get out of my way!"

Our voices were raised to a shouting match.

The door opened and in came Mrs Jones. Peter stood aside in that small room to let her in and I barged past her and through the door. They were taken by surprise and got in each other's way. I shot out into the yard and headed as quickly as I could towards the gate not daring to look back. I was fearful of them catching me and dragging me into the house again.

They shouted to some gardener to stop me but he just stood and gawped. Then they gave up.

"Don't worry Mrs Jones, she is upset by something. Soon as she gets over it, she will come crawling back. She has nowhere to go."

I was free.

Chapter Thirteen

My arrival at the King Alfred surprised a number of people.

"Is this permanent?" asked Alan.

"Yes, I've had enough."

"Right girl, let us get you up to your room and you stay out of sight for the rest of the day." He took me to the bedroom he had reserved for me, gave me a goblet of wine and told me to rest and compose myself.

"If Peter comes I will deal with him."

"Thank you Alan. Will you send John up to me?"

"Certainly."

When John arrived he seemed bewildered. I told him straight out.

"I have left the Manor and your father for good."

"Whatever for?"

"Because I'm tired of working for that snotty-nosed lot."

"What about Dad?"

"What about him. We haven't got on well for a long time and he likes it there. Why did you think I let you stay here with your grandparents?"

That shut him up for a while. I grabbed him and embraced him. He was confused and worried. At last, I would be around to care for him and comfort him in times of stress. There was a lot of lost time for a mother to make up. I burst into tears, which set him off also. We hugged each for a little while. When we came apart and dried our eyes he was back with a question.

"You haven't done this for Uncle Alan have you?"

"No my dear, I did it for me."

After further discussion he kissed me on the forehead and was gone. I hated Peter for making me abandon my son for so long.

Sitting alone in my room I had confused thoughts. Was I right? I could have pulled myself together after the rebuke. Peter's attitude to me had improved of late; he was not so irate and violent as in the past. We should be mellowing after sixteen years of marriage. Why was I here? My whole life had fallen apart. I burst into tears again. I must compose myself before Peter came looking for me.

Soon after I had dried my eyes, Alan appeared and offered me dinner in his room. I was not hungry.

"Come along, you must eat. Perhaps you will feel better then."

I allowed myself to be persuaded because we had to talk.

Half way through a silent meal he asked the key question.

"Are you sure you want go through with this?"

"Yes."

"Things might look different in the morning."

"I doubt it."

"Well if Peter doesn't come tonight he will certainly come tomorrow. Then what?"

"I'll keep out of his way for a couple of days."

"That is alright for the short term, but he will know you are here. You will have to face him sometime."

"I know, but not just yet."

"Alright. If he comes tonight I shall tell him you came then passed on. Tomorrow we will talk about it."

I went back to my room and after a while fell asleep. I woke up in the early morning and lay thinking as I heard people moving about.

I could not go back to the Manor and face their ridicule; a threat had been made, return and so would the threat. Peter's hold on me would be stronger if I 'crawled back'. A bridge had been crossed. Why go back to further humiliation when I had Alan and John to love and could earn my own keep?

I got up and went down in search of breakfast. Alan was there.

"Shall I give a hand in the kitchen after I have had something to eat?"

"Why not? Learn where things are and take your mind off things."

"If my husband comes I will speak to him if he seems reasonable."

Peter arrived in the middle of the morning. At Alan's suggestion, we went up to my room so that we could talk in private.

There came a long, disjointed conversation. He did not see why he had to persuade me to return. It was my duty to go with him. When I repeatedly refused he became irate and began to shout.

There was a knock on the door and Alan came in.

146

"You cannot use my inn to disturb my guests and customers with your matrimonial problems, Mister Jenkins. I must ask you to leave, and stay away until you can behave in a more civilised manner."

I thought Peter was going to attack him but he thought better of it and turned to me.

"You think about what you are doing. I shall come and collect you tomorrow, willing or otherwise!" With that he stormed out of the room and was gone.

Later, as I tried to concentrate on work, I became increasingly concerned with what Peter might do tomorrow. In the evening I sat in the lounge with Alan and John. They both seemed to think that the best way to deal with Peter tomorrow was with violence. This was the last thing I wanted.

"I don't want any fighting. Remember, John, he is still your father. When he comes, tell him I have moved on. I'll hide in the kitchen."

"He might keep coming back."

"Let us get through tomorrow first."

The following day Peter turned up in a foul mood. He shouted and ranted about his rights over his wife. Alan barred him from searching through the inn while I stayed in the kitchen ready to jump into a nearby cupboard if he entered there. I could hear Peter getting ever more angry and threatening. Alan then ordered him out. They squared up to each other. I was very worried. Then Peter stormed out hurling threats at Alan.

"He should get the message now," said Alan.

Later in the day Father Ripon turned up and said he wanted to speak to me. I told Alan I would see him in my room.

There followed a long lecture on behalf of Peter and praise for the Turner family.

"You must swallow your pride and return; it is your duty."

When I stood my ground he changed his tone and began to threaten me with Hellfire. At no time did he ask to hear my side of the argument. Perhaps I might have given way to this browbeating if Alan had not convinced me there was no Hellfire for the sins of one lifetime. Since leaving the Manor I had not committed any sin that I knew of. I told him to go, which nearly gave him a fit, but he went.

That night I crept into Alan's bed.

Next day I started working in the kitchen in earnest.

Then Mrs Jones from the Manor turned up. I had no wish to speak to her. She told Alan what a good husband Peter was and the Turners were a kind, forgiving family and willing to give me another chance in view of my long satisfactory service. Peter was in the lounge listening in and waiting for Mrs Jones to bring me forth. He would have a long wait, I might have been wrong in their eyes to walk out without warning but to go back on their terms would be a fate worse than death.

Before she left Mrs Jones suggested that he should persuade me of the error of my ways. It was his duty. These people always banged on about duty.

"I'll tell her when I see her," said Alan with a straight face.

That was not the end. Before the day was out Father Ripon was back. This time he was talking of the threat of public penance and punishment for adultery. I had seen this happen and it was not a pretty sight; up to now I had thought it right.

Alan was most indignant and swore that I slept in a separate room, was employed as a cook and was a close relative. He demanded an apology. I listened to his words with wonder, nobody spoke to a priest like that. Father Ripon backed down, he was not used to being contradicted. He changed his tune saying it was Alan's duty to return an errant wife to her lawful husband.

"I'll tell her when I see her," was Alan's standard reply.

The priest snorted and left with vague threats.

Alan and I went to bed together rather early that night to demonstrate our contempt for the priest.

I took up the full time duties of a cook before the week was out. Alan paid me the full rate and extra for sleeping with him three nights a week. If I was referred to by various sanctimonious people as a whore I might as well get paid for it. Alan didn't see it that way, he just thought I ought to have a little extra in my pocket for good timekeeping and luring in more customers with my cooking. I had managed to bring away much of the money I had saved in fifteen years as a cook as well.

After Peter had gone with Mrs Jones he did not return. I heard he had been sacked as a butler and had gone off to Bodmin. I prayed for his wellbeing and happiness.

Working at the inn on a market day was heavier than at the Manor. Customers were coming in all the time. A long day round the market made them hungry as well as thirsty.

Once the novelty of my arrival at the inn had worn off, things settled down and ran smoothly.

For the best part of the year, I was happy and all seemed well. Work was hard at times but Alan was a considerate employer and very good in bed. There was no question of being in his bed and just looking at the ceiling. I was encouraged to enjoy myself and sometimes take the initiative, sometimes we got in to some strange and interesting positions. It was never like this with Peter.

We often spoke about reincarnation, he also spoke against the subjugation of women in work and marriage. I had never heard such talk before. He was against the teachings of the Church and the arrogance of priests.

He did not bring his pendulum out anymore.

"We know all we need to know about us; the rest doesn't matter," he would say.

One day there came from somewhere a stranger. He was clean and tidy with bright blue eyes; he was in his thirties, I guessed. The stranger stayed for several days. Alan was quite taken with the man and there were animated conversations between them and several other guests and customers. When the man had gone Alan told me that he was a Lollard. I immediately stiffened up.

"Were not these people in league with the Devil?"

Alan laughed.

"I thought I had taught you not to listen to prattling priests and ignorant gossip. They have a different and more rational view on religion but there is no cause to condemn them out of hand on the say so of bigoted priests. You should listen to alternate views on all things."

I was not convinced. I was glad the stranger had gone. The priest already looked upon us with a jaundiced eye; if he knew we had harboured a Lollard, anything could happen – none of it pleasant.

Then calamity struck. What fools we had been. I was pregnant!

I was thirty-eight years of age; no way did I want a baby, not even Alan's. I would be at risk at my age. The priest and parish officers would come storming in on us. What could I do?

An inn like ours is the centre of the community, all kinds of information and gossip flow through it. There is much to be learned if you listen.

I now listened desperately and made very discreet inquiries there and in the market, and sure enough I heard of a woman in the town who helped a pregnant woman at a price.

It was, in my eyes, starting to show. I talked it over with Alan. Though he was not concerned about the Church, he said I would be the one who would be in trouble and he didn't really want a baby hanging around his inn, so he agreed to pay for something to be done about my condition.

So one day I screwed up my courage and in great trepidation went to see this woman I had been told about. The old crone agreed to help me at more than the going price that I had been told about: she knew I was desperate and Alan had more money than most.

It may have been a relief but was nearly a fatal disaster. I was very poorly after it. For several weeks Alan had to find a replacement in the kitchen; if this went on he might want a replacement in the bed. Another fear was what had happened once, could happen again. What had made me think I was immune to babies?

I needed to get away, rest and think things out. An idea came into my head.

"Alan how far is Jacobstowe?"

"Whatever do you want to know that for?"

"I want to go there. I want to see my father again, and a rest away from here will do me good."

"More likely to kill you off going that far. It's about thirty miles."

"How would I get there?"

"That is a good question; you are in no condition to walk that far."

He thought that was the end of the matter but I persisted and worked out I could get a trader or tinker to take me on the back of his cart for a price. It was suggested that I could perhaps hitch a place on a boat at Newquay and go by sea to within a few miles of Jacobstowe all in one day. The thought of sailing along the North Cornish coast after all I had heard of shipwrecks frightened me off that idea. Alan put feelers out and we found a tinker who had a cart.

Alan insisted that John should go with me. So we set off.

150

The tinker was in no hurry, he had goods to sell. So we rattled and bounced along roads that were worse than the ones to Salisbury all those years ago.

We went via St Columb Major, Wadebridge and Camelford. That took three days. Here, despite an offer of a bonus, the tinker was reluctant to go on and hinted at returning to Newquay to pick up more goods and trade. We had stayed each night in some wayside inns which were rat-infested hovels. John was a big lad for his age and without his presence I might have had trouble from some of the rough-looking men about, for I was still a good-looking woman. The tinker slept in his cart.

While our Tinker was making up his mind, John found a trader willing to take us nine miles up the road to Waithouse Corner for a small consideration. He said Jacobstowe was easy walking distance from there. So off we set over steep hills and muddy roads to the nearest point to Jacobstowe on the main road.

We staggered down a muddy track in drizzly rain into the village which was our final destination. I was by now worn out. I had not been fit when we left Indian Queens, now I felt much worse.

There seemed to be nobody about so we knocked on the door of one of the houses and asked the woman who answered.

"Where does Harold Jones live?"

"Harold Jones?" she asked in surprise. "He died two years ago. What did you want him for?"

I was taken aback: I had not considered such a possibility.

"We have come all the way from Indian Queens to see him. He was my father."

It was the woman's turn to be surprised.

"Father? Would your name be Mary?"

"Yes. How did you know?"

"He told me of you. I'm also his daughter, my name is Jane."

She now beamed on us and took us into her little cottage. I knew none of the names of my father's children by his second marriage but they knew about me.

Jane was a childless widow. She was very pleased that I had come.

"There is no rush for you to go back, is there? You two can stay here as long as you like."

I told her I was a widow too which made John give me a funny look.

Jane ran and told other people in the family and soon I was being introduced to half-brothers and sisters, several uncles and aunts. We were fed and waited on and made a fuss of. Jane gave up her bed for me.

That night I became ill, which was not very surprising. Jane attended to me for the best part of a week. Relatives kept popping in during this time. Though very poorly I felt I was in good hands and felt as though I had come home to my family, which to some extent was true.

Once I was up and about I told John to go back to Indian Queens; I would stay awhile for I would never make the return journey in my condition. John was a fit and healthy young man and said he would be able to walk back in two days. So off he went with a promise to come back for me in four weeks time.

When I was a little stronger, I went to see father's grave. I also found mother's grave. It was rather sombre.

I never knew I had so many relatives and they kept coming along to see how I was getting on and if they could do anything for me.

When I was fit enough I went with Jane to the church at Waisthouse Corner to give thanks for my recovery and for finding my lost family.

All too soon, John returned to take me home. I told him I was not fit to travel and needed a few more weeks rest. Jane and others backed me up and said when I was ready they would escort me back to Indian Queens. In truth Jane and I were happy together and with other members of the family had much to talk about. I thought of Alan and the things he had told me, was he a religious crank? It looked so from here. I thought of Peter also and wondered how he was getting along. I was happier here for the time being but there was a problem. Money was running out. I would have to earn my keep; I could not sponge on my stepsister for too long. The problem was what work was there in a place like this!

"There is some casual farm work to be had," said Jane and one or two others. Jane did this sort of thing and a bit of dressmaking.

"I'm not up to farm work, I'm a cook."

"Don't know about that. You will have to go up to Waithouse Corner and find out what is available in that line, if anything."

So I walked up on to the main road and enquired at the inn. After a few questions on both sides I became cook for the weekends, which was better than nothing and a foot in the door.

I did quite well there, though I didn't like the walk home late at night so one of my half-brothers or Jane would come along and see me safely home. Later I got odd days there as a waitress so things got better, not as good as the King Alfred or the Manor but it was a living.

This went on for quite a while when Jane suddenly sickened and died in my arms. Left alone I cried to Peter to help me. After the funeral I decided it was time to go back to Indian Queens. I discussed it with the family, John had stopped coming to collect me some time before, several years had rolled by without being noticed. It was time to go.

My eldest half-brother Harold said he would see me safely home. So off we went. We walked to Camelford then got a lift on a cart to Wadebridge then walked the rest.

What would Alan say on my return was a growing worry as we approached Indian Queens. What if he didn't want me back? What if he had got another woman?

Chapter Fourteen

As soon as I walked into the King Alfred, I saw Alan at the far end of the public bar talking to a customer. He did not see me at first but when he did his face lit up and he came straight to me. We embraced and kissed modestly. We held each other there in public.

"You're home. You're home," was all he could say.

When we released each other I introduced him to my half-brother. Alan embraced him and shook him warmly by the hand.

"Thank you, thank you, for bringing Mary home safely."

Then I asked him about John.

"He's alright but he doesn't work here anymore. He is not far away."

Harold and I were very footsore, tired and hungry from our walk. We were glad to sit down and rest. Alan brought us a lovely hot rabbit stew that worked wonders on us. Harold was offered free board and lodging until such a time he felt fit enough to walk back to Jacobstowe. I was offered my old bedroom. Alan and I knew it would only be temporary until Harold had gone.

"How have you been getting on with your cook?"

"I've had three since you left, all bad timekeepers, all complain about the work on a market day, none as good a cook as you."

"That sounds like a job offer. Give me a couple of days rest and I will take over, if you are willing."

"The job's yours soon as you are ready."

Harold was well pleased with his stay at the King Alfred. When he left Alan pressed some money into his hand and gave him some food for the journey. I then went down to see my son in his new job and have a chat with him about the family news.

Peter was still at Bodmin and apparently doing very well, there was no sign of a mistress. Mary was still a ladies' maid at the Manor. Kathleen had left the Manor for a better position elsewhere. Joan was working in Bodmin near her father. John, now twenty years old, had his eye on a girl in town.

154

That night I went to Alan's bed and we were back where we left off with all the risks that went with it.

"You won't leave me again as long as that will you?" asked Alan as we lay close together in the early morning.

"Not unless you make me pregnant again. It will probably kill me off."

"I will do my best not to make that happen."

Cheap words not matched by his actions so far.

"Did you have anyone else while you were away?"

Men always want to know that.

"Of course not, though I expect you had more than one lady friend to keep you awake."

"No! No! I only want you. There can be no other."

I had not been back long when I noticed that something different was going on in a small back room from time to time. At first I thought it was some sort of business meeting that was no concern of mine. After such meetings, in which Alan sometimes joined, he seemed animated and willing to talk religion. At other times he would refer to reincarnation.

I became curious and questioned him after one such meeting, half expecting him to say they were spiritualists. Away from his influence, I had had time to reflect and had become sceptical.

"They are Lollards my dear."

I was aghast.

"Are you mad! If you let them meet in here in the King Alfred, the news of it will spread and the Church will be on you. Think of what happened to Oldcastle and John of Sawtry and others. It that what you want, martyrdom?"

"Mary, we must seek truth no matter what the cost, but I believe the Lord will protect us."

"He didn't protect the others!"

"Have faith."

"Are these Lollards spiritualists as well?"

"No."

"Then what are you getting mixed up with them for?"

"We must seek truth and enlightenment."

"You are mad! Get rid of these people before they get rid of you!"

"If a man has something to say about the meaning of life then we must listen."

"We! You count me out."

Things became strained between us when the Lollards gathered in the inn about twice a month.

Alan would still talk about the journey of the soul.

"Be not afraid of death, it is a nothing."

I became increasingly concerned.

Otherwise things went well for us. I had moved into his bedroom on a permanent basis. Alan had heard about the rhythm method from somebody so I was less concerned about being pregnant. Should it happen again we would move more quickly than last time and run less risk to me.

During the 1450s there was much turmoil in the outside world which gave a boost to scandal and gossip in the inns and markets across the land. The English army had suffered a shattering defeat in France. Jack Cade and his rebels had marched on London in protest over something or other and like Watt Tyler's rebels of seventy years before had camped on Blackheath outside London and tried to dictate to the government. There was a lot of animosity in the Aristocracy and it was rumoured that King Henry had gone mad. The Duke of Suffolk had been murdered and his body thrown on the shore at Dover. Then the Duke of York came from Ireland to Wales and marched with a growing army to London to confront the King and his supporters. Everyone felt the country was going to the dogs.

Sir Samuel and a number of his retinue had ridden off to London to join the turmoil but nobody was sure whose side he was on. Indeed many changed sides as they saw fit. Into this turmoil came bands of unemployed soldiers from France, willing mercenaries. Us ordinary people did not want to get involved – what we wanted was peace and prosperity regardless of who was in power. But it all went to give our customers something to gossip about.

Alan continued on occasion to talk of our past life together and our future life. I didn't like the idea of being a fisherman so I tended to let it all go in one ear and out the other.

The meetings of the Lollards became a regular thing, which was their undoing. The Church got to know in advance when these meetings would be held and decided to strike when they were all gathered together.

One evening I was in the kitchen preparing a meal, Alan was in the backroom with the Lollards when I became aware of a lot of shouting and tramping about. I poked my head out the door and got the fright of my life. The place was full of armed soldiers from the Manor, parish officers, and priests; most of them shouting orders and threats. A number of people were being frogmarched away. Most went quietly murmuring prayers, some shouted and struggled. Alan was one of the latter. I fled back into the kitchen, all a tremble. What should I do? Father Ripon and another priest with an armed soldier suddenly appeared in the kitchen.

"Put those fires out and go home. This establishment is closed forthwith!"

Everyone ran round in fear and excitement. As cook I set about putting out the kitchen fires accept one small one, I might need that. There was nowhere for me to go, this was home.

Father Ripon came across to me.

"You Mary Jenkins are under arrest for aiding heretics and witches and for adultery!"

The blood froze in my veins.

"You will not leave this building without my authority on pain of death. You will not consort with heretics and witches. You will be questioned about your activities later; until then, stay here. Understand!"

I nodded my head for I was incapable of speech.

The building was rapidly emptied of people. Outside a hostile crowd was milling about.

I sat down in the lounge in a state of shock. I was at the mercy of sadistic fanatics who would do God knows what to obtain a confession and information on others, particularly Alan.

I contemplated suicide and flight. How? Hang myself? Cut my wrists? There were people outside watching in case I left.

I began to pull myself together and went round making sure all the doors were secure, I tidied the place up and then went into the kitchen and picked up a carving knife. I stood for a moment then my courage failed me. A voice in my head whispered,

"Be not afraid, all will be well."

I was in such fear for myself and Alan that no tears would come. That night there was no sleep.

In the morning I had a small piece of bread and some wine when there came a banging on the door. I hurriedly unlocked it before it was broken down.

Soldiers and priests, with the town constable, pushed in past me and began ransacking the place, some went into the small backroom that the Lollards had used.

I stood by the door full of dread. Then I became aware that Father Ripon was looking intently at me. He moved across towards me, slowly, full of malicious intent.

"Mary Jenkins I have spoken to the Bishop about you. You are to leave here for your own safety. I shall take you into my protection in the Rectory. I also will be responsible for the initial questioning. So come with me."

Like an obedient subdued dog I followed him out of the inn and up the road to the Rectory. People were standing about watching, some made nasty remarks; a soldier came with us to keep the people away.

There was a cellar in the Rectory. Father Ripon led the way down the narrow stone steps, followed by me, then the soldier, with the curate bringing up the rear. Father Ripon had brought a torch with him that he fixed to a bracket in the wall of the cellar. The flickering light cast weird shadows on the walls. There was a wooden stool in the corner. I was told to sit on it. Before I knew what was happening a manacle on a chain fixed to the wall was snapped onto my left wrist and locked.

I almost fainted. Then I screamed. Chained up down here anything could happen. I pulled on the chain but only cut my wrist. I wet myself then burst into tears.

"Let me go!" was all I could say.

"Scream as much as you like," said Father Ripon. "Nobody can hear you down here."

They all turned and filed out the door and back up the steps. Father Ripon removed the torch from its bracket and followed them. When the door clanged shut I was left in total darkness.

I leaned on the wall and sobbed my heart out. I prayed like I had never prayed before.

I don't know how long I was left in the dark; it seemed like years. To add to my horror I could hear the occasional movements of rats or whatever. I cried, I prayed I dozed, I screamed when I thought a rat was near.

Then the door opened. Father Ripon came in holding a torch aloft and looking down on me. Then one of his minions came in with a jug of water and a plate of food that was set on the floor beside me. The minion went out and came back with a latrine bucket which he set down within reach.

Without a word the door was slammed shut and I was in total darkness again. I gulped the water down but never touched the food. At last I stood up and took a few steps, I went only four short paces then the chain stopped me. I sat down on the stool again and tried to keep calm, it was very difficult. I lost all sense of time in that dark, horrible place. I tried not to think of the things that could happen to me now I was a prisoner.

Why didn't I use the carving knife when I had the chance?

The door opened and woke me from a doze. Father Ripon came in alone, he put the torch in the bracket then closed the door. He came over to me and stood there towering over me in the flickering light, a figure full of menace.

"Good, I see you have eaten." I looked down at the plate. It was empty, the rats had had it. I shuddered at the thought of their closeness.

"Now Mary, I must ask you some questions. You must answer with truth for other investigations will reveal if you lie. My wish is to help you in your predicament, and save your immortal soul." His voice was soft and silky. "I know you are a whore but you once were a respectable wife and mother. You allowed yourself to be led astray into wicked ways. I must save you." He stood looking down on me and I cringed.

"First of all Mary, are you a Lollard?"

"No."

"Have you joined with others in reading of the Bible?"

"No."

"Do you know or have you met any Lollards?"

"Some used to come to the inn but I never spoke to them."

"Then how did you know they were Lollards?"

"The inn keeper Mister Mills told me."

"Ah, Mister Mills is he now? Is he a Lollard?"

"Not to my knowledge."

"Do you believe in the Father, the Son and the Holy Ghost?"

"Yes."

There followed some more questions about Lollards then he changed the subject.

"Are you a witch, Mary Jenkins?"

"No."

"Have you attended covens and rituals with witches and warlocks."

"No."

"If you lie you will surely be found out and things will be much worse for you."

There was another change of subject.

"Mary Jenkins have you committed adultery?"

He knew the answer but it seemed to give him pleasure to bring up the subject which Alan and I had once strenuously denied.

"Yes."

"With how many men?"

"Only one. He said it was not adultery because I was his common law wife."

"Adultery is adultery."

I was suddenly aware that he had moved much closer.

"Do you realize that if there is any doubt about your answers you will be put to torture to extract the truth?"

"Yes."

"Did you or your friends commit evil acts, such as bestiality, group sex, sodomy or fellatio?"

"I have heard of group sex but I have no idea of the other things you mention."

"Are you saying you don't know what I mean by fellatio?"

"I have no idea what it is."

"Then I will show you."

There it was: his rampant member in front of my face.

God please help me now!

He stroked my cheek with its gleaming head, his hand entwined in my hair to pull my head forward. I knew what he wanted and my life could depend on it so I closed my eyes and did it.

He stayed awhile after he was satisfied, stroking my hair and my face saying nothing. Then he went leaving the torch behind to give light to my abode. I felt terrible and wished I could die there and then.

I think it was the next day when Father Ripon returned bringing a jug of water but no food. He asked much the same questions as before until he came to the adultery bit. Then he stroked my hair I thought we were going straight into the same as yesterday.

"If I take you out of here do you promise not to try and escape?"

Out of here! It sounded like music. I nodded vigorously. I was willing to do anything at all to get out of this festering black hole.

That set him off to perform the same act as before. This time when he had had his way he unlocked the manacle and helped me to stand up. Going up the stone steps was a difficulty but at the top I was rewarded with daylight and sweet fresh air. He took me to a small bedroom that was more like a cupboard and told me to rest. I stood by a small window sucking in the fresh air. I was too tired to cry. I was in the hands of a sexual pervert and there was nothing I could do about it. I lay down and immediately went to sleep.

I don't know how long I slept but I was woken by Father Ripon who had brought me some food and wine. I was feeling hungry for the first time since the Lollards and Alan had been seized. I ate all the food, drank the wine then lay down to sleep again.

When I awoke again it was dark except for the light coming through the window. In this dim light I made out the figure of Father Ripon. He was naked. Without a word he slipped into bed with me and did what he would. At first I gritted my teeth and lay stiff as a board, then I realized this would not do. If I did not respond and cooperate I could face fearful trouble, so I set out to maximise his pleasure as Alan had taught me. He was there several hours, we said little. Then in dawn's early light he kissed me passionately, got up, and was gone. Just like that. I hated him.

During the day I was well fed and allowed to use the outdoor privy.

At night Father Ripon was back in my bed. I forced myself to respond and he was pleased.

The next day Father Ripon had me brought into his private room. He said it was for further questions.

"Tomorrow you will be taken to Bodmin for questioning by the Bishop. If he is not satisfied with your answers you will be sent to Exeter."

He then reeled off a list of questions I was going to be asked and the most suitable answers to give if I wished to avoid a trip to Exeter.

"Remember them, and look subdued."

We went over the questions again, then with the questionnaire in my hand I was left to my own devices for the rest of the day. Father Ripon did not come to my bed that night.

I was beginning to feel a bit more confident of my survival.

We were off early the next morning. I don't remember much about the interrogation by the Bishop but I survived with a warning. We returned to Indian Queens with an admonishment to attend religious instruction with Father Ripon, he also added his warning.

"You are under probation so don't draw attention to yourself. You had best stay at the Rectory until we find you somewhere to live."

"I will stay with my son for a while."

"Very well. Your first session of religious instruction will be in three days time."

I stayed another night at the Rectory so that Father Ripon could collect his reward in bed.

With Father Ripon's permission I was allowed back into the King Alfred to collect personal belongings and change my filthy dress. I wandered alone through the ransacked building. My savings in a wooden box under the bed were gone as were other items of value. Then I saw Alan's little wooden box with the pendulum still in it. The priests had not recognised the significance of the pendulum otherwise Alan would surely burn. I took it away with me.

Alan – what had happened to him? Would he be executed? I asked Father Ripon but he told me not to enquire about any prisoners unless I wanted to draw attention to myself.

I left the King Alfred with a bag of essentials and went down to John's cottage and sat on his doorstop until he came home.

"God, mother you look awful. I have been worried to death over you." He took me in to his cottage and gave me something to eat. He bade me stay at least a night. I hugged and kissed him. He did not ask what had happened since I had been taken out of the King Alfred. That night I had the best sleep since this horrible affair had started.

The question was what now? I had no money, the King Alfred had been closed down, I could not expect to find decent work as a suspected heretic. Father Ripon said I could not leave the parish. John told me to stay with him until I decided what to do.

Father Ripon insisted that I turn up for religious instruction. As I expected I was the only one there. He laid me across the table with my skirt well up so that he could feast his eyes on me before thrusting away.

"I must leave the parish," I said when it was all over.

"You are not allowed."

"I must if I am to earn a living, nobody will employ me here. I have nobody who can support me for long."

"Then come to the rectory and cook and housekeep for me and the curate."

How could I refuse! I was not required to live in. I got no regular pay only the half pennies that Father Ripon felt like giving me now and again, but I got my keep. What he called 'religious instruction' took place at least once a week.

I felt depressed, degraded and befouled. How could I end such a situation?

John and others commented on my woeful looks and poor health.

The following year the inn was put up for sale by the parish authorities. Alan had fled the country.

I went along one day to enquire who had bought it. I got the surprise of my life. There surveying the building with two other men was Peter!

He saw me and came straight over.

"Mary! How are you?" He kissed my hand.

"Can't complain I suppose," I smiled weakly at him.

"You don't look too well. Where are you living now?"

"With John."

He said a few words to his companions, then insisted in coming with me to see John. We had a long conversation, with John in the background. When he left he said he would like to see me again next time he was in Indian Queens. He and his two companions were thinking of buying the King Alfred. It was going cheap.

Over the next few days John said I was looking better. I also found an excuse to miss 'religious instruction' on the grounds of ill health.

Peter came back a week later and took me over to the King Alfred. I wandered all over the building with him and his partners. I showed them around the kitchen and living quarters, including my old bedroom.

At the end there was whispering between Peter and his friends, then Peter came over to me.

"We would like to offer you your old job of cook, when we open."

I was speechless for a while.

"We think you are the ideal person, if you are willing."

"Yes I will think about it. Would you expect me to live in?"

"Yes. I know we are legally married Mary, but I promise not to molest you in any way."

The sudden thought of sleeping with him again after the monster in the Rectory was not repulsive. I was beginning to feel for him again.

He gave me some money which he said was an advance of pay; he knew I was hard pressed.

Soon after that I moved into the King Alfred to help get things organised. I couldn't believe my luck. Then another blessing fell on me. Father Ripon was moved to a larger parish. I was free!

'A good man like him would be needed at a more important place!' they all said, and wished him well. I wished him to hell.

Though we were husband and wife we kept our distance at first, some new people did not even know we were married.

We worked hard to rebuild trade and re-establish our customers.

Peter and I steadily warmed to each other again. He was different to the Peter I knew. He was a gentleman and had a positive cheerful approach to all problems and ideas. Not at all like the obnoxious whinger I had left.

After a few months, as everything was going so well both in the business and in our private lives, I decided to try my luck after we had been drinking more than usual. I took the plunge. I entered his room, took off all my clothes and slipped into bed with him. I wanted my conjugal rights back.

From here on there was no looking back.

John and Peter got on much better together. Joan also turned up and we all agreed she should work with me in the kitchen. Mary also paid us a visit as the news of our reconciliation got round. Kathleen was the last one to come along and wish us well. We did not have much spare cash at first, and we had payments to make to Peter's partners who had paid the biggest payments to get us started, but we steadily built up our reserves.

All round it was like coming out of a nightmare. As time went on the relationship between Peter and I bloomed, I was a much more experienced woman and he was more of a gentleman. The years rolled on and all was well.

A civil war broke out between the aristocracy and their supporters but here in Cornwall all we got was gossip and slander about the contenders.

Then on 25th of March 1459 I was going down the cellar steps for something when I tripped and fell headfirst all the way down. I broke my neck and died on the spot with one brief cry. I was fifty-one years old.

It all seemed strange at first but my two mothers and my two fathers were there to guide me.

PART 3

Chapter Fifteen

I was not much in favour of being born into a sixteenth century fishing family in south west England but I was persuaded that was where I would find souls that were at the same level of the journey as I was and people I knew already.

So I was born as Adam Simpson on the 4th March 1514 at Lynmouth in Somerset. My father Horace, born 1490, owned a small fishing boat which gave him a decent living for the times. My mother Olive nee Hunt was born in 1491. They had been married in March 1510 and their first born, Horace, had arrived three months later.

By the time I arrived they had two daughters as well. Two years after I arrived they had another daughter, Iris.

We lived in one of a row of cottages which were all full of fisherfolk. Built on the side of the hill we would watch all the boats coming and going in the harbour.

In my early years I yearned to go on a fishing trip with my father and elder brother Horace. It seemed a wonderful life though I did not like the smelly fish they brought ashore. Fishing for herrings just off shore seemed to be the main occupation in the village and nearby Lynton. Being a closed sort of community nearly everybody was related to everybody.

Though I had been on several joy rides on my father's boat it was not until I was eight years old that I went out to earn my living catching fish. I was taught by my father how to cast a net, how to haul it in, and how to watch for a sudden change in the weather that could bring disaster. That first day brought an end to my childhood. I was elated. I was fascinated by the sea view of the coast, a most pleasing view, better even than the land view of that wonderful coastline.

When not out fishing there were nets to mend, the boat to maintain as well as odd jobs expected of a boy who was no longer a child.

Like all seafaring people, we were very religious and attended church as least once a week.

169

Iris was the baby of the family and everyone seemed to think she was wonderful. I thought she was spoilt and selfish. Horace and I got on well enough, though from time to time he would try to put me down, which could end up with an exchange of blows. I got on very well with Sylvia who was a year older than I. Though I looked up to my father who was a hard working, hard drinking cheerful chap, it was my mother who I thought was wonderful. She seemed also to favour me, which Horace would comment on. There was something undefinable about the woman. She was a good homemaker and cook but she seemed to know more than most people, especially the other women. I worshipped her.

A seafaring life for offshore fishermen is a healthy life, not like it was on great journeys and cramped sailing ships ruled by bullies. We just bobbed about in sight of land, caught fish and built up a huge appetite for when we came ashore. As we grew older we developed a raging thirst to go with it that could only be quelled with a jug of cider. Father said it was the best life there was and would continue as long as there was herring to catch off the Somerset coast, which he thought would be for ever. He was not concerned with the future or the outside world. What wonderful days they were.

I soon learnt where the hidden rocks were and the sandbanks along the coast. We knew the coast like the palm of our hand. We sometimes went down into Bideford Bay in search of a shoal of herrings, and sometimes we disposed of our catch across the Channel in Wales. The Welsh were not good fishermen so we got a better price. We did not do that very often for it was a long way to go in such a little boat; anything could happen in mid-channel and once there the wind could stop you getting back when you wanted to.

When I was seventeen we had a big family celebration for the double wedding of my two older sisters, Heather and Sylvia. Everyone from our community turned up for the party including a sixteen year old girl by the name of Mary Holt from a few doors away whom I had known all my life; her father was also a fisherman. From now on, I took a much greater interest in this Mary Holt and before long we were always together when we got the chance.

Fishing was a family business for all of us, and the two girls getting married set me thinking. The proceeds from fishing were a family income but when a young man got married, what then? What would happen if Horace got married? Would he get a bigger share of the catch to support his wife and possible children?

I raised the problem with mother when we were alone.

"No problem," she said. "A young man starting married life will need a boat of his own, and his family and friends would build him one."

Within months the truth of this was demonstrated when father, Horace and I gave a hand in building a boat for a newlywed couple. When it was in the water we all had a lovely party and for the first time in my life I got drunk. The logic of this was that there would be more boats with every generation, but would the fish increase at the same rate? It was not a question to raise openly in a place like Lynmouth.

One question I did raise with mother was would people help me build a boat when I got married if they had recently built one for Horace.

"Are you thinking of getting married soon to Mary Holt then?"

"Good Lord no! I was just thinking it might be difficult to earn a living when I get married to whomever."

"No 'whomever' about it, you will marry Mary Holt. Not only is she a fine, decent girl but you two are destined for each other."

"What makes you say that?" I was interested in Mary, it was true, and we had got to the kissing and cuddling stage and we saw a lot of each other when I was ashore and neither of us were busy. But mother was jumping the gun, 'you are destined for each other', what an odd thing to say. However I let it drop this time.

My courtship of Mary continued slowly for a couple of years but it progressed. As mother would say, I was the thinking, serious chap of the family whereas my father and brother were doers.

After a while I decided to question mother regarding my destiny as she called it. Even though there was less crowding in the cottage with the two girls gone it was still not easy to have a private conversation without interruption. I decided the best plan was to wander down when she was on her own getting water from the well. I kept my opening light-hearted.

"Have you heard anymore about my destiny, Mother?"

"I know all about your destiny my boy."

"Well don't keep it a secret, I at least ought to know."

"Can you keep a secret?"

171

"Of course I can."

"I'm not talking of tittle-tattle secrets, but profound things with wide implications."

"I think so." Mother was not always this serious, What had happened? There was a longish pause as though she was gathering courage to go on.

"Do you believe in reincarnation?"

"What is that?"

"Do you believe we all have a soul?"

"Yes, of course."

"Do you believe in Hell and Damnation?"

"Yes."

"Why?"

"Because the Church says so." What a funny set of questions.

"What if the Church is wrong?"

"Whatever can you mean? How could the Church be wrong?"

"I mean that what if there is no Hell? Nobody has ever seen it. What if God is not a monster that casts people into fire for eternity?"

"God is not a monster. What you say is heresy, mother."

"What if you were given another chance here on earth to mend your ways and pay for your sins?"

"Another chance?"

"Yes. That is reincarnation."

"Do you believe that?"

"Yes."

We were interrupted at this point by other people coming to the well.

We went our separate ways. She had me worried. Mother would never make up such a story. She would never knowingly tell me a falsehood. What had come over her?

It was a couple of days before I could catch mother alone again at the well.

"Regarding what you said the other day. If you do not believe in God and Hell, why do you go to church?"

"One cannot stand out against a community or a family when they are convinced they are right. Children need the guidance of religion and the example of their parents. Spirit and contemplation can be found in a church more than in most places. You are not a child, you must think for yourself and not let others do it for you."

I didn't want to hear her going on about the Church. I brought the conversation back to where I wanted it.

"Why did you say that Mary Holt and I have a destiny together?"

"Because you have been married twice before at least. You have something to work out together."

I was dumb struck for a moment.

"How can you know this?"

"My son I will tell you if you promise never to tell anyone else. Do you promise?"

"I do."

There was a pause while she decided how to start.

"I have a pendulum which takes me back in time. I know who you were in a previous life and who I was. I must go but I will tell you more later."

She left me standing there gawping after her like an idiot.

If mother had a pendulum that told her about past lives then she must be a witch. Had the Devil got to her? Should I tell the priest so that he could save her? I thought I ought to tell Mary, which indicates just how close we had become. We had moved on to being lovers and knew without saying that we would soon be married. We wanted the timing to be right and to have things settled before we openly said it, though everyone knew the way things were going.

When next I got mother on her own I wanted to know how far this thing about the pendulum had gone.

"Does Father know about the pendulum?"

"No."

"Don't you think you ought to tell him? He is your husband."

"He would not be able to cope with it. He might even take it off me and throw it into the sea."

"That is a good idea."

"Don't talk like that. It is a wondrous thing. It can reveal many things to our advantage."

"Have you told Horace?"

"No. I have told nobody but you. I have told you because I think given a little time you will believe. You must tell nobody, no matter what the circumstances. You are the only one I can confide in."

"Where did you get this pendulum from?"

"A woman who is now dead. She gave it to me the day she died and told me how it works."

173

"How long have you had it?"

"About two years, but I have only used it in the last two months. It has told me so much."

"What has it told you?"

"Well first of all, you in your last life were a woman, you were called Mary Mills but that was not your real name. You married a man called Peter Jenkins in 1428 when you were twenty-one. You worked in a big house. You left him for a while for a lover but then you got back together later. Peter Jenkins then is Mary Holt now, which is why I know you two were meant for each other."

"What happened to the lover?"

"He fled because of religious persecution."

"Perhaps the lover will come back in this life."

"He already has."

We stood looking at each other for a while. Then, as before, we were interrupted, for several families used this well: the women found it an ideal place for a gossip. So I left mother with our neighbours.

Mother was having delusions and I couldn't see how I could help. Then I got another problem when I met Mary. She was pregnant.

I was glad to escape to sea with Horace in the afternoon. I was sorely tempted to tell him about mother but decided I had enough problems with Mary. The moment I said anything about mother's condition it would open up a whole world of problems and mother would be in serious trouble, for people gossip. I decided to talk her out of her delusions. She got in first.

"My son I know you are worried and confused about what I have told you. Let us put it to the test. I will forecast an event that has yet to happen then you will know the pendulum tells the truth. Also you ask me a question I cannot know the answer to and I will get the pendulum to tell me."

I decided to humour her.

"What then is your prophesy?"

"The King will shortly defy the Pope and set himself up as Head of the Church in England, the new queen will be executed within two years."

"Mother you not only speak of heresy but treason also! The Pope would never allow it!"

"What is your question?"

I had to think hard. Then I came up with three questions to mother, which only I and Horace knew the answer to – and Horace at this moment was at sea with father.

"I will need ten minutes or so; come and see me for the answer at home then." She went off with her bucket of water. I wandered along the hillside and watched our fishing boat a couple of miles out before I went to see mother.

To my astonishment mother answered all three questions perfectly.

"Let me see this magic pendulum of yours?"

"You can see it but never touch it." She took me into her bedroom and produced a small wooden box. Out of this, she lifted a pendulum in front of my face.

"There is a tremendous knowledge and wisdom here I have only just started to understand it. I notice you and Mary will be married on your twenty-first birthday. How nice."

I was stunned, Mary and I had not made any decision about the date and had not definitely said we were to wed.

It seemed that this pendulum of mother's had strange powers.

Chapter Sixteen

Mary and I, because of her condition, decided to get married in June 1534. That would demolish mother's forecast. When I told her the date that we had planned, she said "We shall see."

No sooner had we announced the date and begun preparations than Mary told me it was a false alarm. She had lost the baby before it had been noticed, there was no longer any reason to rush. We decided to stick to the date anyway. But fate was not to be denied. Mary's mother fell seriously ill and as the only daughter at home it fell to Mary to nurse her. She asked me to put the date back until her mother was better or whatever. The weeks dragged on into months.

"Don't worry boy, all will come right on your birthday," was my mother's claim.

It seemed a long way off and I saw a lot less of Mary at this trying time. I was hoping to break the forecast and end mother's obsession with the pendulum.

Then I had a troublesome thought, the lover of Mary Jenkins in the last life might reveal himself. Mother had said he was already here. I had a feeling that he might come between Mary and I. I decided to seek him out first.

"Mother how is your pendulum of late?" I asked her one day at the well.

"It is fine. I don't use it too often, but it's fine."

"You told me that in my last life I was a married woman and I had a lover."

"Yes that is right my son."

"This lover is here and you know who he is. Tell me then who it is."

"No need for you to worry about your past love. This time he is an older woman."

"An older woman!"

"Yes."

"Do I know her? Tell me who it is?"

"No I won't."

"Why not?"

"There is no need for you to know."

Afterwards I wondered about my sanity for holding such a conversation.

In the outside world there was in 1534 a major event that was to affect the whole country.

King Henry decided to break with the Pope. The proclamation was read out from the church pulpit. Copies were nailed up everywhere for the literate to tell their friends and relatives. From here on the King would be the head of the church as far as England was concerned.

Mother smiled and nodded to me when the news broke.

It set the village and no doubt the country by the ears. There was animated chatter that at times became noisy and threatening. Though most people were Roman Catholics there emerged a strong assertive element in our midst. Then came the Commissioners with a Royal Warrant and armed soldiers to reorganise the Church and remove things of value and stamp on what they called idolatry.

There was quite a commotion around the church, the priest was persuaded to go along with the new order if he wanted to keep his job. He then set about calming everybody down. Other priests elsewhere would not submit to the Commissioners and were removed under threat of arrest. Some went into exile, some into retirement, others who were indiscreet went to prison. All in all, there was a great upheaval and nothing was ever the same again.

Mary said she was glad our wedding had not gone ahead amid such disruption.

Just before Christmas, Mary's mother died. It was a relief for two reasons. It put an end to the poor woman's pain and misery and it released Mary to think again of marriage.

We discussed the matter and decided not to wait until the Church had settled back into its old way for that could take several years. Mary would probably fall pregnant again before the Church sorted itself out for we were once again seeing each other more regularly.

"The springtime will be a nice time. Why not on your birthday?"

"Have you been talking to my mother?"

"No, why?"

So mother's pendulum was still working after all.

Despite the upheaval in the Church our wedding went forth as mother said it would. Life could not stop because clerics, kings and popes had fallen out.

Some said it was not our quarrel, some said reform had improved the marriage ritual, some said it would not be a real marriage. We got on with the practicalities of the situation. After all it was the same God they were arguing over.

We had luck when it came to where we would live: Mary's father decided to go and live with his eldest daughter in Lynton as soon as we were married. As regards a livelihood I decided I would stay a fisherman which meant the building of a new boat, one which could be handled by one man but bring home enough fish to support a family. That would be no problem.

So as mother's pendulum had forecast I was married on my twenty-first birthday on 4th March 1535. We had a great party afterwards and to loud cheers I carried my new bride across the threshold of our new home.

We were left in peace for a couple of days which was just as well as our minds were concentrated on sex. Then Horace came knocking on the door. It was time to build a boat. As usual there was much hilarity and drinking, at my expense, as we worked away. A wonder it floated. But float it did and accompanied by several other boats I set off on a maiden voyage. It was a tremendous feeling. I had my own boat which gave me status in the community as well as independence. We splashed about for an hour or more, nobody caught any fish. Then I was back to Mary and the pleasures of the flesh.

Religious troubles or not these were good times. Clever people talked of the King's wicked devaluation of silver coin; we didn't care, we didn't have any.

Before you could say 'Ahoy'! Mary was pregnant. This time she did not lose it and in December our firstborn son arrived, we named him Horace after my father.

I did not trouble about mother and her pendulum at this point in time. If she was using it, it seemed to be doing her no harm. Anyway, most of the clergy who might have got nasty were taken up with their own quarrels and had little time at present for the sins of their parishioners. Church attendance seemed to decline as the two sides fought it out. Then came news that some top people were being burnt alive by the King for setting a bad example to the people, whatever that meant. It was unsettling.

The following year was even more unsettling. The Commissioners appeared with their Royal Warrants at all the abbeys in the land and closed most of them down and seized all their wealth and lands. Monks and nuns were out on their ear. Top people squabbled over the spoils. How could God sit by and watch robbers, despoilers and the profane attack his Church? But he did.

Something else happened in that year of 1536. Queen Anne was executed!

I went to see mother when I heard the news.

"Your pendulum had turned out right again."

"What else would you expect. Have you told Mary of the pendulum?"

"No."

"That is good. Too many people know about it and the witch-finders will swarm all over the village."

"You have never told me who my lover was in my last lifetime. Who is it?"

"Do you really want to know, my son?"

"Yes."

"Does that mean that you believe in my pendulum? Believe in reincarnation? Believe in karma?"

"Yes! It has been so right on everything. I cannot dispute the Christian Church is in decline. Does it also mean the end of the world?"

"No."

"But that still doesn't answer my question."

"You will not stop asking until I tell you, will you?"

"No, even if I have to get my own pendulum."

"Very well. Prepare yourself. Alan Mills, your cousin and lover in your last life, was I."

I stood motionless with mouth wide open as this sank in. Mother walked away.

Later that day I went to see mother and insisted that we have a long talk where we could not be interrupted. We decided the best place would be in my boat on a calm day because mother was not up to rough seas.

We soon had a nice day, Father and Horace had disappeared along the coast towards Minehead on a fishing trip. Then with mother on board I set off in the opposite direction. I had the advantage of wind so I would sail along easily with out much effort. Father had tacked along the coast so that when he was loaded he would have an easy run back to Lynmouth. Once settled, and mother had spoken about the pleasure of cruising along off the coast with seagulls screaming at us and a warm sun shining down on all and everything, I opened up the conversation on the topic we had come here to discuss.

"Now mother, you have persuaded me of the existence of reincarnation and Karma. That we know many of the people around us from previous lives. If you were my cousin and lover, and Mary was my husband, who else is in this life who was here before?"

"In your last life your father was your foster mother, Edith Mills, who raised you from a baby when your real mother died. Your brother Horace was your foster father. As I said, I was your cousin Alan Mills, who was your cousin and lover for a while. I have not found any sign of your sisters yet but I think they are there somewhere in your past. It is not essential that we all be born together every time."

I mused on this for a while as the gentle wind pushed us towards Bideford Bay.

"So we have come together again as family and friends. Why?"

"It is so that we can help each other in our spiritual journey." She paused and gazed for a while at that beautiful sunlit coast. There were other boats about with our friends and neighbours on board all going about the business of earning a living.

"I found out last week we had met before our last life, we were illicit lovers then. You were an English archer at the siege of Calais and I was a young French widow. We had two children. Your name then was Thomas Simon." It sounded embarrassing and a bit like incest between mother and son.

"It means we need not fear death, it is but a change of form. A place where we rest and assess what has gone and what we should aim to do in our next life."

"But we still don't know why we should all come together here in this life in this place."

"It is to strengthen our bonds and love for each other so that we may be fit to move on to higher things. It is essential therefore not to harbour ill will or animosity to anyone, least of all our companions on

180

our eternal journey. We must, if we wish to progress, love and help everyone otherwise we are not fit souls. We must bear malice and envy to nobody."

I could think of nobody to whom I bore ill will.

"Have you looked into our future?"

"That is more difficult because I am not sure what question I should ask, the pendulum only answers questions. Going back in time seems to flow without too much trouble but there is the problem of finding time to do these things. When I go forward I find there is much death, I don't like that. I know when most of us are going to die."

I didn't want to know about such things and we fell silent for a while.

"I do know you will have three more children and your brother Horace will never be married."

"Where will all this end?"

"When we have learnt to love and help all we meet, then we will be ready to move on and never return to a human mortal life."

We were now opposite Combe Martin. More boats passed by. Most of the occupants hailed us as we passed by. Probably they wondered what a middle-aged woman like mother was doing in a working boat.

"I think we ought to go back. I must be there when your father returns: he is always hungry when he comes back from fishing, and your brother is worse. You were also when you lived at home."

I hauled the boat round and began to tack towards Lynmouth, this required more concentration and work.

"Does Mary feed you well?"

Mothers always seem to ask this question of their newlywed sons.

"Of course Mother. Sometimes too well?"

I changed the subject.

"What do you think of this religious quarrel. Is it the end of the Christian Church? Will a new religion develop? Are you in favour of all these reforms?"

"Yes I am in favour of reform. The old religion stopped people thinking for themselves; it led them to believe all sorts of stupid things. If people can be excused their sins by a priest for a sum of money then the whole thing is a mockery and a rip off. The new

181

religion will open up people's minds. In time they will think in terms of the spirit and a better world will emerge as a result."

I listened as best I could as I worked the boat and the wind sighed in the sail. It was rockier going back against the wind and we shipped a little water.

"But don't you think the new people are going about it the wrong way, the top men seizing Church lands and the state taking other property? It is antagonising the people and causing chaos."

"We have to live in the real world. The powerful people were bound to go too far as regards property, though the long-term result is to the good. Queen Anne was executed because she objected to the stealing and squandering of Church wealth when it could have been used by the state for the good of the people. That was her belief. If the state had taken it all, Henry would have only used it to finance war. The King needed to let his supporters plunder the Church to gain their support against the Pope. The Church had gained most of it by deception anyway."

"I have noticed you don't go to Church as much as you did before the King took over."

"I don't need to. I support the Church of England but your father and most people do not. Why should I incite dissension when it cannot last. Nothing that is imperfect can last and the reforms are imperfect."

"Imperfect or not if they find you in possession of that pendulum they will charge you with witchcraft and you know what that will mean."

"I know, Son, which is why I only told you."

We came to Lynton and I ran the boat ashore. I kissed mother goodbye as I helped her to clamber out onto dry land.

"Take care mother, there are evil people about."

"I know. See you later."

I watched her go off towards home. I was filled with love for her and a great up lifting of the spirit. If things were left to mother and her kind then all would be well with the world and the human race would progress to much better times.

Chapter Seventeen

Then Mary fell pregnant again. The child born in 1537 was a boy we called Samuel. What more could a man want than two healthy sons? I went along to mother to persuade her to find out if I had met my boys in a previous life. For some reason she was reluctant to find out.

"It's not a suitable time or place to continue with the pendulum, there is a risk of being found out every time I use it," was her plea. I suggested another trip in my boat. She said no. I don't think she liked the idea of anybody being able to see her when she used her pendulum, including me.

Then one day when I saw her alone at the well I approached her to press the matter.

"I have found out who your second son was," she said before I had spoken a word.

Tell me."

"He was your mother's brother by the name of George Davies. He lived in a place called Jacobstowe, You did meet him. I can find no trace of Horace."

"Thank you mother. Now tell me, will my two boys survive childhood, for many are at risk in their first years."

"Do not ask such questions!" she snapped at me, then picked up her bucket and went.

Why should she be annoyed, the answer might enable steps to be taken for their safety. Then the reason slowly dawned on me and I was dejected.

From there on I watched my two sons like a hawk for any sign of illness or weakness. Then Mary fell pregnant again. This time we had a little girl that I named Edith after my foster mother in my previous life. I didn't tell Mary the reason for the name.

Once again I asked mother if Edith and I had met in a previous life. The answer was yes. In my previous life she had been my only son John. Once she told me this I reopened the previous question.

"Mother I have thought about what you have said, or didn't say about my children surviving childhood. I have a right to know which of them is at risk. I am their father."

"You have no right. You have a duty. Should anything fatal befall them it is not the end of the world. It happens to all of us. Just care for them and love them."

"So it is true that one or more of my children will not live to grow up."

"I'm saying nothing." She stumped away with her bucket.

After that I did not see mother for a little while. I heard she was very insistent that father and Horace go to church with her every week at least.

Was it a good thing to know events in advance? Knowing about things in the past was interesting and enlightening but, as mother said, 'ahead was death'.

Then came bad news. Horace and Heather contracted smallpox along with other people in the district. Horace was one of those who died; we were all shaken. Horace had been a fit active young man. Heather was left scarred for life. We worried about each other for some weeks for nobody knew who would be next. We had tended to think of this disease as confined to crowded, dirty cities but there was nothing to stop it travelling with traders etc.

Then in January my dear wife Mary contracted it. I refused to leave her; mother took the children away at great risk. Did she know something we didn't?

After being very seriously ill, Mary slowly got better, though like Heather she would be marked for life. She was worried about what the children would say about her face when they saw it; in fact they were so pleased to be home that they never commented on it. To assure her that the scars were not important I made love to her. Only the once but it was enough to make her pregnant again. Almost immediately our eldest boy Horace, only three years old, caught the disease and perished in April that year. We were devastated. In my grief I foolishly blamed my mother for not warning us. What good was a warning of a disease that appeared here and there across the nation. She also had lost a son and had turned to the new Protestant Church in her grief. Mary accompanied her. Two deaths in the space of a few months were hard to bear. But bear it we must as life flowed on.

The next three years was a time for recovering from the shock. Father now, like me, fished alone. We had several times thought of combining but it would mean me joining him in his larger boat. I consequently would have less income, status and independence. I had grown used to working alone on my boat; father was not, he sorely missed Horace.

The controversy over the change of religion seemed to have died down in our area: the heat seemed to have gone out of it. How little did we know.

I did not bother mother too much about her magic pendulum and she told me little. I had toyed with the idea of getting my own pendulum but abandoned the idea. I knew why we were here and about previous lives, the future I did not want to know after the loss of a brother and son. In any case mother said there was a ritual to go through to activate a pendulum and she was not prepared to tell me, in any case we had no idea if it would work with any pendulum. Mother did say on her deathbed she would give me the pendulum and the secret of how to use it.

Despite heavy inflation and religious disruption, I made a steady living at offshore fishing. I noticed that father had slackened off his efforts, he only had himself and mother to support whereas I had a wife and three children. Our last child Martin had arrived at the end of 1539.

In the summer of 1542, mother started to go to church more often and began to look a bit depressed. I recognised the symptoms.

I made a point of catching her alone at the well.

"Mother dear, there is something troubling you. Is it something you have learnt from the pendulum?"

There was a longish silence.

"Is someone in the family going to die?"

She stiffened up and I saw a tear on her cheek.

"Yes my son. I wish I had not looked into the future."

"Who is it?"

"Your father will die in October."

"Is there nothing we can do?"

"If his time has come it has come."

"Do you know how it will happen? Will he be taken ill or what?"

"I dare not ask."

"Well if you did we might be able to do something about it."

"I don't believe that. I shall be left all alone."

"You will never be left alone, mother."

"I can't live with my children, they have their own families to think about. I shall be on parish relief, what little bit that is."

"Pull yourself together mother. The first thing is to find out when, where and how this thing will happen, then perhaps we can do something."

Mother went off with a vague promise to consult the pendulum.

I went several times that week to persuade her; she made all sorts of excuses. Then she came along to my cottage just as I was leaving to do some fishing and walked down to the boat with me.

"I have done what you said."

"What is it you have found out?"

"Your father will die at sea on the 24th October."

"Well there is the answer then. We must make sure he cannot go fishing on that day."

She seemed to brighten up at that.

"Another way is to tell him what you know."

"He would never believe me."

"I don't see why you can't get him to believe; you made me believe."

"You are different, as I said before. We will do better to say nothing but prevent him from going to sea."

So mother went home happier and I had a good day fishing.

Over the next few weeks we thought up various plans to prevent father from going fishing on the 24th of October. The best plan was a family party for the day with a bonfire in the evening. Thus father would be held safe in the bosom of his family and the power of the pendulum broken. Being October it might be too rough for him to think about going out anyway.

On the day in question mother kept father busy all morning, then in the early afternoon people began to come along. Mother and I helped to keep him busy and well-oiled enough to keep the idea of fishing out of his mind. Our plan was working as the afternoon wore on, there was eating, drinking and singing and the bonfire was stacked up ready and still growing as the afternoon wore on, the weather was quite good.

Jimmy Potts was there: a relation of ours a year younger than I. He had a lot to say to father about his new boat. We left them to it.

186

As the weak sun slipped towards the horizon there was a sudden sharp squall. Mother without reason got agitated at this moment and ran into the house ahead of everyone. Father and Jimmy were not there.

"Don't panic mother, I'll go and find them."

"Something has happened, I know it has!"

I headed off towards the harbour; father was probably there looking at Jimmy's new boat. Rain was falling and it was coming over dull with scudding clouds. I saw Jimmy bringing his boat in.

"Where is my father?"

"Out there!" He pointed to the harbour mouth.

"What the hell do you mean?"

"I took my new boat out to see how it went; your father came along in his. A small squall hit us at the harbour mouth as we turned back. I think he had a bit of trouble and we got separated."

"Turn this thing round!" I grabbed the gunwales of his boat.

"It is dangerous out there."

"That is why we are going!"

We turned the boat around and set off across the harbour. Outside the entrance I could see no sign of father's boat. The rain had stopped and the wind had fallen, it had only been a short squall. The light was starting to fade. We tacked along the outside, other boats had joined us sensing something was wrong.

Then there it was! Tipped up and crashing against the rocks. I was all for closing in on the wreck. Jimmy flatly refused. I abused him for being a coward, swore at him and punched him, but he would not go close enough for me. Other boats came alongside. These rocks were dangerous and in the failing light nobody dared close in. We called until we were hoarse. There was no sign of father. Perhaps he had scrambled across the rocks and was safely ashore.

It was dark when we returned. Mother was devastated: all her plans to save him had come to nought – the pendulum had won.

The next couple of days we searched along the coast on sea and on land. Some even climbed down the face of the cliff to the boat. The sea and the rocks between them were breaking it up. There was no sign of father.

Mother brightened-up rather quickly over those two days.

"It was fate, it cannot be denied. He is happy and safe now."

People thought she was a little touched but I knew what she meant.

The disaster seemed to frighten Mary. Up to now she had not worried about me going to sea, but if father, a very experienced sailor could be lost at the harbour mouth, what risks was I taking?

I went along to mother and asked the key question.

"How long have I got? Will I be lost at sea also?"

"No my son. You have many years to go yet."

How could I convince Mary of that?

Even if I was at risk there was no other occupation around here that would give me an equal living. I was bred to the sea, but promised I would not take any chances.

All went along as normal after we got over the shock. My son Samuel grew into a healthy, active boy and before long agitated to come along with me for some fishing. The prospect worried Mary but what alternative was there? I said I would take him along with me in the spring of 1546; to stay longer than that would make him a butt for his friends and be upsetting for him. The autumn before, I hauled my boat ashore and got down to some serious maintenance and alterations, as much to assure Mary as myself.

One day I was working on my boat when my brother-in-law Hubert, husband to my eldest sister Heather, came along. We talked awhile then he examined my boat and asked questions about my plans. Then he watched me working for a while.

"You know Adam, you would be better off making boats than sailing them."

He was a boat builder at Minehead.

"Repairing a fishing boat is not the same as building lots of them," I replied.

"See one fishing boat and you have seen them all. It is a safer job and you earn more."

"Are you making me a job offer?" I asked light-heartedly.

"Well actually, yes. Trade is building up, I have only one man with me, I need another and you look like the chap I want."

I stood and looked at him. I had never in my life thought of doing anything else than offshore fishing. This idea required thinking about.

"You make up your mind and I'll be back next week. Let me know yes or no then."

The idea grew on me. Being a boat builder at Minehead did not mean I could not sail my own boat for pleasure. No smelly fish, no hauling nets, no risks from sudden squalls. No worry for Mary.

I stopped work and went to talk to Mary.

She had grown sombre over the last few years: the smallpox marks depressed her, she was worried about the risks I was taking and now there was the prospect of Samuel also following me to sea. One more had been lost to the sea only a few weeks back.

When I told her what Hubert had said she was much in favour, even if it meant us moving to Minehead. I had to admit that the idea appealed to me as well.

What about mother? A son has a duty to look after his mother. I went to see her.

"How is your pendulum, mother? You haven't mentioned it lately."

"I don't use it very much these days."

"Well how about asking it a question for me?"

"Past or future?"

"Future. Hubert wants me to go and work in his boatyard at Minehead. What can your pendulum tell me about that?"

"Come back tomorrow and I will tell you." Now that she lived alone she had more freedom with her pendulum.

So I went back next morning and she was waiting at the door for me.

"Yes, you and your family will be happier and better off at Minehead."

"But what about you, mother?"

"Tosh! I shall be alright. I'm fifty-four years old and have lived here all my life. Why should I move?"

Hubert returned and we agreed I should start working for him in the spring. In the meantime I would go alone and live at his home while I built myself a house at Minehead.

So after Christmas with my boat now ready I set sail on a good day for Minehead about fifteen miles along the coast.

Chapter Eighteen

I settled into boat building work quite well. The boats were bigger than those I sailed in, with more sail. The man I worked with, Martin Jones, was a friendly helpful type, about my age with a pretty wife some ten years younger. They had no children; we cannot all be blessed. Hubert was also very helpful but he was often away advancing the business.

Mary and the children were in the house that I and Martin had built close to Martin's own which stood on property owned by Hubert. Hubert and my sister lived further away in a better part of the town.

Mary and I were quite happy with our new life. There was no more coming home cold and wet smelling of fish, there was no more heaving on the nets in a rocking boat, no more worry about the price of fish when you got it home.

Hubert was more interested in getting things right than in doing more work per day. He did insist on proper organisation and preparation before work began so that work flowed easier. Most of the boats we made were to order; we were slowly driving out the individual builder.

The social life was more alive than at Lynmouth for there was more than just fishing going on. Trade was passing through to Wales and Ireland: wool, hides, cattle and coal as well as herrings brought ashore by people I often knew.

Samuel was a sturdy lad of nine years, old enough to earn his living, so I got him a job in a carpenter's yard, Edith too was put out to work. Martin stayed at home until the end of the year because Mary thought he ought to learn his letters. So he spent time at an elderly lady's house with other boys learning not only to read but write as well; then he was put to work.

During this year Martin and his wife Hilda, who was nicknamed Missy, set about teaching me to read in our spare time. In Lynmouth we had not bothered with such things but here, in a bustling place like Minehead, everyone said such skills would come in handy.

190

The year was 1546, a year of settling in for me and the family; we had to adjust to new jobs and new faces. Mary was at first reluctant to go out amongst strangers with pox scars on her face, but got over the reluctance as the year wore on. I would at first always accompany her to give her confidence.

To my surprise I found that Hubert and Martin were in favour of the Church Reformation and would often break into discussion on the subject. I adapted somewhat to this position to keep the peace. I knew the old Church desperately needed reform, the people were entitled to something better than what the Pope and his minions were offering, but the present reformation was being used as a screen for greedy unprincipled men. I dared not speak of reincarnation. They assumed I was a Puritan which I was not. Not that they objected to Puritans, they looked upon them as cranks, so I came in for some lecturing.

I decided, at their suggestion, to go along to Bible classes. There, sections of the Bible were selected for reading and discussion. We ended up with prayers and hymn singing. Ten years ago we would have been dispersed and some arrested for heresy. What had been heresy then was rapidly becoming orthodox now. What strange times!

1546 moved on to become 1547 and in that year the King, who had set off so much controversy, died. We now had a sickly boy of nine on the throne. It was soon shown that he was under the control of Protestant Lords who were intent on pushing the Reformation forward. The arguments for and against intensified as the nation's leaders prepared their plans. I was increasingly drawn to the new order of things and also the reading of the Bible, which I found very difficult, but Martin and his wife and occasionally Hubert would enlighten me according to their interpretation. At least there was always interesting people to meet. On Sundays I would go to the parish church with Mary and the children. Once a week I would go to the nearby tavern with Martin and sometimes Hubert. The conversations were eye-opening. Many and varied were the men in the tavern, all willing to express their opinions on every subject under the sun. Right now politics and religion were the favourite topics.

Another thing that happened to my family coming to Minehead was we were drawn into the money economy. We had hardly bothered with it in Lynmouth, now it was all important and I began to gather some with the children working and boat building being a cash only industry.

In the early spring of 1548 an old fishing friend turned up from Lynmouth with a message. Mother was ill and wanted to see me as soon as possible.

Against Mary's wishes I sailed down the coast to Lynmouth, she wanted me to walk along the coast. She was frightened of the sea. I found I was much out of practice with my sea sailing but got there alright.

Mother, when I found her, was with Iris. She did not look at all well and was having difficulty breathing. After a brief chat mother said she wanted to speak to me alone, so others withdrew.

"My boy I said I would leave you the magic pendulum. Get it out." She indicated a box in the corner. I rummaged through it and brought forth the small box containing the pendulum.

"Open it up boy and take the pendulum out." She had difficulty wheezing these words out. Not only was she ill, she was at the ripe old age of fifty-nine.

I pulled it out and dangled it between my fingers, then painfully and slowly she explained what I must do before I could use it.

So the pendulum was mine, a magic door to the past and the future. I hid it away before the others came back in. They were very curious about what mother had said but I kept quiet.

Within a couple of days mother had started to pick up. Soon she was well on the mend, I said goodbye and took off to Minehead on the first favourable wind.

Back at Minehead when I was alone I took the pendulum and looked at it closely, then I went through the ritual to activate it for me alone. I was a bit worried about asking a question but if I didn't ask how would I know it was working. If mother had asked the question it would have told her she was not going to die and I wouldn't be in possession of it. I asked the question that mother should have asked. The answer was that she still had until 1556, eight years away. I then took the plunge and asked how long had I got. The answer was that I had until 1567, nineteen years away. That was enough for now, I put the thing away.

The following year was a year of upheaval. The Government had decided there would be a Prayer Book which would lay down the rules for all churches.

Out was to go church painting and vivid colours. Gone the mystique of the Mass, glowing vestments and the awesome moment of the elevation. Gone the ancient vessels and shrines decked out with the generosity of generations.

The churches now looked empty, whitened and cold. No longer was it sufficient simply to be there. The congregation was required to learn new prayers and responses and to listen to the Bible read in English. The Act of Six Articles left over from Henry's day had been repealed the year before. Now in July there was the destruction of all images and idols. When Bishops did not comply they were removed. The lectern and pulpit replaced the alter. No longer was God a remote and awe inspiring being. Man could approach God without earthly intermeditaries. The priests had lost the key to heaven.

Most people though baffled went along with the new regulations with varying degrees of alacrity.

Only in the South West, Cornwall and Devon did the confusion and controversy manifest itself with open revolt.

A host gathered and marched east in growing numbers to lay siege to Exeter. They sent a petition to the Government, the old rituals to be restored, the Prayer Book to be laid aside and the English Bible be withdrawn'. The Governments response was to crush the revolt with force. Thousands died.

One day in this time of trouble, work was a little slack so with agreement Martin went off to a religious meeting. Hubert went off on business and I took a day off. It was a warm day. I told Mary I was going fishing. On the way, for no known reason, I popped into see how Missy was.

I found her sitting just inside her doorway wearing a very flimsy dress. She got up when I arrived and moved back into the house. Missy and I had always got on well together since the first day we met and she had been very helpful in getting me to read. She was an attractive woman with auburn hair and a pleasant figure. In contrast Mary was over weight and scarred. We looked at each other and something happened between us.

"Would you like to come on a little fishing trip with me Missy?"

"Not in that boat of yours. Two of us rocking about in that little thing would soon turn it over."

'Rocking about.' The term gave me a boost. There was a twinkle in her eye. We moved closer.

"I have a day off. What would you like to do?"

"Martin won't be back until sundown so you could say I have the day off as well."

There was a mischievous look in her eye. A small voice told me it was time to run out of here but I was losing control in face of her delightful figure and those welcoming eyes. We moved closer.

"It is a hot day. One should not run about and get sunstroke. If you have the day off, relax. Get some of these heavy clothes off." She began fiddling with my clothes. Before you could say 'Praise the Lord' we were in each other's arms kissing with passion and joy. We were pulling off each other's clothing. It did not take long. Mary and I had not had sex for several weeks; it appeared Missy was in the same condition. I laid her across a strong table and with her strong young legs around me drove straight into her. It was over too soon, a moment of ecstasy. A smooth youthful face and big smile to go with it. Mary and I always made love in the dark because she was conscious of her scars. We took a little time to disentangle ourselves, we didn't want to give up. The door was still open, anybody could walk in and catch us so we straightened ourselves out.

"You must come here more often," she said in a silky voice.

"I will." At this point I had no pangs of guilt.

I went off for a little fishing. I dozed off near the harbour entrance and caught nothing; after all, it was a hot day in more ways than one.

From there on taking my pleasure with Missy was a difficult thing that required organisation if people were not to get suspicious. Martin did not go away to religious meetings very often for my liking. However we still managed to have sex about once a fortnight. Being forbidden fruit and dangerous made it much more pleasant.

For Missy, she said it brought her sex life with Martin to a complete standstill. He did not seem to mind. For Mary and I, it gave us a boost: while waiting for the chance to get at Missy again I indulged myself with Mary. All women look the same in the dark. Mary was well pleased.

Things rolled on happily like this into the new year.

Then one morning in bed with Mary she came out with a surprise.

"Missy does not have sex with her husband. She must be very frustrated. She fancies you."

"You women talk about some funny things."

"If you made a pass at her you would get an instant response. Think of those lovely breasts at your command."

"Give over Mary. It is wrong to covet another man's wife."

"Don't go all religious on me, Adam Simpson. Sex was invented before prattling priests, who apparently have been making hay with virgin nuns while telling us to behave."

I got out of bed quickly. I was embarrassed and concerned that this hinting at Missy hid some knowledge.

From chatting discreetly it appeared that Missy wanted children and Martin could not give her any which was why she wanted me. Then I thought, why hasn't she become pregnant? After all we had been making love for a long time now. The answer was that it wasn't Martin that was impotent. Missy was barren. For a woman in that condition she was doing well. It stopped me worrying and stepped up our relationship. I was able to satisfy two women, neither aware of the activities of the other, or so I thought. The situation continued for a number of years, we all seemed so friendly and happy.

The Protestants were now in full charge of the Church and state and they decided to end the controversy over the Prayer Book by producing a new and more radical one. The Reformation was growing by the day. This was not to last.

In 1552 the young King, who had never been a strong lad, died. After a usurper had been stopped, Mary Tudor became Queen. She was openly determined to roll back the religious reforms of the past two reigns; those who resisted would be burnt at the stake. The first to go was a chap named Thomas Bilney. Other followed, including the ex-Archbishop of Canterbury. She also made an unpopular marriage with a foreign prince, Prince Philip of Spain. Sovereign and people were on a different course and lives were lost.

At this time of worry about people being burnt and killed, and the Church changing back to Popish hands, I was distracted by a quarrel that broke out between Hubert and Martin. The root of it was the falling off of work. This quarrel went on for several months with each side trying to embroil me. The end came when Martin decided he had had enough and went off to pastures new taking his sexy young wife with him.

Mary astonished me some weeks later when she said.

"I'm glad that whore Missy has gone. I know about her and you. I think she was having it off with Hubert as well. May she rot in Hell!"

I was too stunned to make an immediate reply. When I did it was so feeble and transparent that she quickly demolished my protests.

"If you believe that why did you not say so?" I asked.

"I knew it would not last. You were mine and always was and will be. If you go off the straight and narrow I must accept that is what happens when a cheap harpy flaunts herself. I love you, you are mine forever regardless of others."

What could I say?

It was in this same year of 1554 that our only daughter started courting a presentable looking young man. Before you could say 'Hold on' he was asking for her hand. I had been forewarned by Mary and we agreed they seemed suitable. So when he came around I hummed and puffed before I gave way. Then just before the wedding in December Mary told me our daughter was already pregnant by about five months. I had not noticed until it was pointed out to me. I had too many distractions that year. It was just as well I had given my consent.

Edith seemed very happy with her married state and in March 1555 she gave birth to a little boy. She caught some infection and in great pain died. She was sixteen years old. We were completely shattered for a while, but life goes on.

In the aftermath, I decided it was time I had another look at the pendulum.

Chapter Nineteen

I had not told Mary about the pendulum. To avoid questions I went out in my boat across the harbour on what was supposed to be a fishing trip. Here I took the pendulum out of its box and set about asking questions concerning my family. Most of the answers seemed satisfactory. Then I checked on Mary and found she still had seven years life to go which would leave me on my own for five years. I made a promise to myself that I would make her last seven years happy. The time with Missy now seemed a sordid chapter of my life, totally out of character. Or was it?

Then for some unknown reason I looked at Hubert's life destiny. To my surprise he only had two years left. That did not look right, he seemed quite fit and I knew of nothing that was wrong with his health. But if that is what the pendulum said, I could not doubt it for it had always been right.

The question then was what would happen to my livelihood if Hubert died and the building yard closed. The answer came back that I would be an offshore fisherman again. I found that a bit depressing. To start back at that work in my forties was not a happy thought. But what will be will be.

I returned to shore and Mary asked on my arrival home why I had brought so little fish.

"You are getting past it old man. You would never earn your living at it now."

"Oh yes I could. I was out for pleasure today. If ever I had to put my mind to it I would go beyond the harbour and bring back a load of herrings."

"In your dreams."

I did not enlighten her.

With only me at the yard all the time and Hubert only occasionally, I was kept quite busy. When Hubert was there he was full of chat but I think he was worried about the viability of the yard and the rising level of inflation.

When work was slack I worked on the renovation and maintenance of my boat. It needed it for it was getting old. I knew that before long I would have to rely on her again. There were more tools in the yard than scratching about at Lynmouth. I was quite pleased with my efforts. When I had finished it I sailed it out of the harbour to get my sea legs back. I did not tell Mary for she always worried when I was at sea; she thought I was pottering around in the harbour.

With Missy gone, Mary and I got on much better; her scars were also fading.

"Hidden by wrinkles," she would say.

I decided to check back on our relationship through past lives. I found we had been married at least twice before. I had been the wife for thirty-one years last time. In the fourteenth century I had been her husband for thirty-six years. Mary was right, we were meant for each other. There was no trace of Missy.

I went down to Lynmouth two days before mother died, everyone was surprised at my arrival for nobody had sent for me.

"Look after the pendulum it can give you warnings of trouble if you ask the right question," she said when we were alone.

"Yes I know mother."

"Has it told you when I will die?"

"Yes mother."

"Will it be soon?"

"Tomorrow."

"It is well. I have had enough. When it is your turn, pass that pendulum on to your children; it will give then an advantage in life. I only wish I could have persuaded your father."

After she died I went home for a while then returned for the funeral.

Mary was frightened at me being at sea but a son must pay his last respects. Hubert would bring Heather along behind me in his boat. In fact they never arrived. On my return I found Mary much agitated.

"They have arrested Hubert!"

"Whatever for?"

"Heresy."

"Oh God no."

Officials from the parish, the state and the Church had come for him, others searched his house. Some even searched the empty house that had been Martin's home.

"They want to talk to you as well."

The thought of jumping into my boat and fleeing out of reach passed through my mind to be dismissed immediately. That way I would have to leave Mary behind for my boat wouldn't take two people on a long sea journey. Where would I go? Why should I flee? I had done nothing wrong. I was not going to the stake that was sure. Well not for another twelve years anyway. Anything could happen before then if the recent years were any guide. I decided to sit it out.

Next day they came and took me away to the vestry for questioning. If it went wrong I would end up at Wells with Hubert. It was a three hour ordeal. While it was going on, they searched my house. It emerged that they were not concerned very much with me, they were looking for evidence against Hubert. I pleaded ignorance. After all I was only an ex-fisherman that happened to work for him. Eventually they let me go. Mary burst into tears when she saw me.

The next few days were a worry for us all but most of all for my sister. News came that Martin had also been arrested.

The Catholics were out for revenge and hoped to re-establish their control over the community. It was no way to run a Christian Church.

Heather went off to see Hubert at Wells. She came back in a pitiful state. He had defied them and been tortured; if he continued to defy them, he would burn.

So that is what the pendulum meant.

Martin on the other hand had recanted and admitted his sins. They released him.

Despite my assurance, Mary was terrified that I would be arrested and thought up various plans to hide me.

My problem was to earn a living. The boatyard was closed down. I had no choice, I was back to fishing. I told Mary I did not need to fish to any great extent, there was only the two of us to keep.

I found to my dismay that a boat load of herrings did not at the end of the day bring in the price I expected. I would have to go to sea more often. How did young fishermen with families to keep manage? They must spend more time at sea than I ever did.

Times were not good.

At Heather's request I went to Wells to entreat Hubert to recant before his trial. I went by boat to Weston then walked the twenty odd miles to Wells. I stopped overnight at the village of Cheddar. Once I was in Wells I had no trouble finding the prison where Hubert was kept near St Cuthbert Church. I had no trouble getting in to see him either.

He was in a shattered state in a filthy, dark hole. He had been racked and could no longer stand. He was not the only one there. He was pleased to see me and asked about all the folks at Minehead. After a little light talk, I raised the subject which I had come here for.

"I cannot recant," he replied. "It is the Lord's will. I must be true to the Lord."

"The Lord does not want you to die. It is pointless."

"How do you know?"

"I know more than you think, much more." I wished I could tell him about the pendulum but knew it would alter nothing; he might think I was a crackpot.

"Is that so? Are you a Protestant still?"

"Yes, more so."

"Then you should be willing to lay down your life for your religion, your children and your country, I am."

"You being executed will avail your family nothing."

"I will save my soul and set an example. What is a little fire against eternal life."

"You have eternal life already, you don't need to go through this." I could see I was having no effect on him. He was a very brave man; it was his destiny to die shortly, the pendulum had said so, but he didn't have to die like this. I left him for a while to fetch some food and fresh water. I tried to keep my eyes away from the other shattered figures around me and Hubert's injuries. If this was Christianity then the sooner it was swept away the better. I stayed with Hubert as long as it was allowed. The authorities didn't mind people seeing the Hell they were responsible for, it might frighten others to conform. In fact it did no such thing and the tally of brave people rose as that terrible reign dragged on.

I stayed the night in a tavern in Wells then walked the whole way to Weston where I fell in my boat and was asleep in a minute.

I was depressed and worn out when I got back to Minehead. There was no way I could comfort Heather. She decided to go back to Wells for the trial.

Once the short trial was over they didn't waste time. Hubert was burnt alive the next day. Heather fled the scene when the fire was lit.

She returned to Minehead a week later. At least she had her house to live in. She was an emotional wreck. Mary and I amongst others would often go up there and try and cheer her up.

While I struggled to earn a living, the torture and burning went on and more and more people wished Mary Tudor to Hell where she belonged.

In 1558 Matthew, now in his twenties, brought home a young lady he wished to marry. The wedding was fixed for November. In fact it was a double celebration for as the wedding began the news arrived that Queen Mary had died. The priest was annoyed because we could not contain our joy. We had a new Queen – whatever she did she could not be as bad as the monster that was now dead.

The boatyard that Hubert had owned never opened again, I tried for other jobs in boat building for I got satisfaction from the job, but being in my mid-forties I stood no chance against younger better-trained men with connections.

So fishing it was.

I continued earning my living from the sea and every time I came into harbour there was Mary waiting for me with a big smile. We were happy together in those last years, then she died as ordained at the age of forty-seven. I could not see why she had to leave me after twenty-seven years together this time round. I loved her and needed her. One should be thankful for small mercies I suppose.

Once the funeral was over I had five years to find a new owner for the pendulum and persuade them of its power. Matthew was the obvious choice of the two; he was married with children, Martin would never have any. The other two of our children had preceded us to the grave.

I had to work out a plan, for Matthew was the practical type and would need a lot of convincing.

I invited him to come alone to my cottage for a private chat on an important matter. When we were settled in my parlour with a flagon of cider in our hands I opened the conversation with.

"Do you believe in reincarnation?"

He didn't know what the word meant until I explained it to him.

"I have never given it serious thought," he said giving me a funny look. He thought I was getting old and frightened of death so was trying to convince myself of a replay. The discussion went on for a long time. I got him to take it seriously before I showed him the pendulum. The old form of question and answer was played out over the next three or four weeks before he was convinced. I had then decided it was not enough. The idea of reincarnation must be spread; mother had wanted that but had done nothing, so I would. I went along to Martin and Heather and slowly persuaded them of the survival and return of the spirit. Heather was most responsive and it cheered her up no end, she would see her darling Hubert again. I told them to spread the word but they did not have much response without a pendulum. The fact that I had spread the knowledge made me feel that my life had been worthwhile. Why had I not told Mary? In this earthly realm I still had to earn a living. I longed for a chance to stop fishing for it was wearing me down.

I was in the garden digging the ground over on 14th March 1567 for some spring planting when it happened.

There was a violent shaft of pain going right through me which stopped me crying out. I was dead before I hit the ground. I was fifty-three years old.

There was a moment of confusion then my mother and Mary were there and took me by the hand. We went to meet several spirits we had known before in the last life and before.

In the last three lives I had betrayed the one I loved, I had broken marriage vows and been weak. We agreed we would have to do it again until we got it right. There was not much point in hanging around when we knew what we had to do. We decided to be born into a widespread family that could give support. I was to be born as a female in what humans call the early seventeenth century.